# A Candlelight Ecstasy Romance™

## IN SPITE OF HERSELF, AMANDA STARTED TO RESPOND

. . .

She felt as if she had been thrust into a giant ocean of desire and was drowning in dangerous excitement. Her body ceased all sign of protest to melt against his as she surrendered to dizzying waves of enjoyment, the slow burning fire only he was capable of igniting, conflagrating into open flame. . . .

# CANDLELIGHT ECSTASY ROMANCES™

38 SUMMER STORMS, *Stephanie St. Clair*
39 WINTER WINDS, *Jackie Black*
40 CALL IT LOVE, *Ginger Chambers*
41 THE TENDER MENDING, *Lia Sanders*
42 THE ARDENT PROTECTOR, *Bonnie Drake*
43 A DREAM COME TRUE, *Elaine Raco Chase*
44 NEVER AS STRANGERS, *Suzanne Simmons*
45 RELENTLESS ADVERSARY, *Jayne Castle*
46 RESTORING LOVE, *Suzanne Sherrill*
47 DAWNING OF DESIRE, *Susan Chatfield*
48 MASQUERADE OF LOVE, *Alice Morgan*
49 ELOQUENT SILENCE, *Rachel Ryan*
50 SNOWBOUND WEEKEND, *Amii Lorin*
51 ALL'S FAIR, *Anne N. Reisser*
52 REMEMBRANCE OF LOVE, *Cathie Linz*
53 A QUESTION OF TRUST, *Dorothy Ann Bernard*
54 SANDS OF MALIBU, *Alice Morgan*
55 AFFAIR OF RISK, *Jayne Castle*
56 DOUBLE OCCUPANCY, *Elaine Raco Chase*
57 BITTER VINES, *Megan Lane*
58 WHITE WATER LOVE, *Alyssa Morgan*
59 A TREASURE WORTH SEEKING, *Rachel Ryan*
60 LOVE, YESTERDAY AND FOREVER, *Elise Randolph*
61 LOVE'S WINE, *Frances Flores*
62 TO LOVE A STRANGER, *Hayton Monteith*
63 THE METAL MISTRESS, *Barbara Cameron*
64 SWEET HEALING PASSION, *Samantha Scott*
65 HERITAGE OF THE HEART, *Nina Pykare*
66 DEVIL'S PLAYGROUND, *JoAnna Brandon*
67 IMPETUOUS SURROGATE, *Alice Morgan*
68 A NEGOTIATED SURRENDER, *Jayne Castle*
69 STRICTLY BUSINESS, *Gloria Renwick*
70 WHISPERED PROMISE, *Bonnie Drake*
71 MARRIAGE TO A STRANGER, *Dorothy Phillips*
72 DESIGNING WOMAN, *Elaine Raco Chase*
73 A SPARK OF FIRE IN THE NIGHT, *Elise Randolph*
74 CAPTIVE DESIRE, *Tate McKenna*
75 CHAMPAGNE AND RED ROSES, *Sheila Paulos*
76 COME LOVE, CALL MY NAME, *Anne N. Reisser*
77 MASK OF PASSION, *Kay Hooper*

# A FIRE
# OF THE SOUL

*Ginger Chambers*

*A CANDLELIGHT ECSTASY ROMANCE*™

Published by
Dell Publishing Co., Inc.
1 Dag Hammarskjold Plaza
New York, New York 10017

Dell ® TM 681510, Dell Publishing Co., Inc.

Candlelight Romance™ is a trademark of
Dell Publishing Co., Inc., New York, New York.

ISBN: 0-440-12540-5

Printed in the United States of America
First printing—September 1982

*For Annie and Florence*

To Our Readers:

We have been delighted with your enthusiastic response to Candlelight Ecstasy Romances™ and we thank you for the interest you have shown in this exciting series.

In the upcoming months, we will continue to present the distinctive, sensuous love stories you have come to expect only from Ecstasy. We look forward to bringing you many more books from your favorite authors and also, the very finest work from new authors of contemporary romantic fiction.

As always, we are striving to present the unique, absorbing love stories that you enjoy most—books that are more than ordinary romance.

Your suggestions and comments are always welcome. Please write to us at the address below.

Sincerely,

The Editors
Candlelight Romances
1 Dag Hammarskjold Plaza
New York, N.Y. 10017

# CHAPTER ONE

"I love her, Andy. I don't know when it happened, or why—but I do."

Amanda raised her forehead from its resting place against the steering wheel of her car, the topaz beauty of her darkly fringed eyes swimming with tears as she stared unseeingly at the unfamiliar terrain. The simple words echoed once again.

"I love her, Andy. I love her—*her*!"

Long tapering fingers tightened as they lay curled in her lap, the nails digging unmercifully into the tender flesh of her palms. Marla! Her sister! Only recently turned eighteen and pretty as the proverbial yellow Texas rose. Carl loved Marla!

At first she had not believed it. Carl was going to marry her—Amanda. Everyone knew it, just as they knew that the sun would rise in the east each morning over the small farming and ranching community of Kemperville. Carl Douglas was going to marry Amanda Reynolds. It had been accepted by family and townspeople alike from the time the two of them were twelve and ten respectively.

All through school they had been sweethearts, and afterward she had taken a job at Kemperville's only bank in order to save enough money, so that when they eventually did marry, she would be able to help Carl with his farm. That she had risen from the starting position of filing checks to teller to manager of the loan department was an added bonus. It was only from the position of hindsight that she could see it had all been for nothing.

Possibly at twenty-five she should have been more a woman of the world—seen what was happening, been prepared. But she had not. The news had come with shattering surprise and it had taken all the courage she possessed to pretend she was unaffected. To act as if she, as well, had outgrown the childish relationship that had been allowed to drift and was happy that Marla and Carl were engaged. And she had to be convincing, for she knew that small towns are a universe unto themselves, with gossip the lifeblood.

But for a novice to give an award-winning performance for a few days, a few weeks, is one thing; carrying it on indefinitely is another. Amanda knew she would have to leave and grasped at the first straw that presented itself.

As long as she could remember, she had loved sketching scenes in pencil, doing pen and ink drawings, watercoloring, and even toying occasionally with oils. But she had enjoyed her talent only as a hobby, devoting herself instead to long hard hours at her job, adding to the growing nest egg in her account—not realizing that both the money saved and her well-known love of art would combine to be a means of escape.

When Carl came to talk privately with her, to try to explain his actions, she had countered with the good news that her father's brother, who happened to be a very successful and nationally known artist, wanted her to come live for the summer on his ranch in the hill country of central Texas, where he would coach her. She told Carl that he had seen some of her work and thought her talented enough to possibly make art her life's work just as he had.

It was all a lie, of course. Her Uncle John had never seen

anything she had done and it was at that particular moment the idea of going to his ranch occurred. But as the days went by and people for miles around heard the news of Carl and Marla's engagement and dropped by the bank to gently—and in some cases not so gently—question her, the idea grew and solidified.

She had placed a quick call to her uncle, not going into detail with him, just asking if she could visit for a while, and received a warm affirmative answer—the only problem being that he would be out of town for the next couple of weeks. But he told her to come anyway and make herself at home. His housekeeper, Mrs. Hazel Gowen, would be more than happy to look after her. It would give the woman an opportunity to bully someone other than Boyd, his foreman.

Amanda loosened the pressure of her fingernails against her aching palms and blinked forcefully to clear her eyes.

She didn't want to come here—but then she hadn't wanted to stay in Kemperville either. Especially not when Carl's words kept repeating themselves in her mind as clearly as if he were sitting next to her and not over two hundred miles away.

The thought of continuing to work in the bank, with all the memories as to why she had taken the job in the first place, was more than she could handle just then. She had turned in her notice, rejecting the bank president's plea that she take only a leave of absence, and burned all her bridges behind her.

Aunt Margaret, her father's older sister who had raised Amanda and Marla from the time their mother died, had considered her foolhardy in the extreme, chiding her repeatedly about leaving such a good job that certainly wouldn't be there when she returned.

Her father had said nothing. He only gathered her into

11

the circle of his arms and held her long into the night, sitting curled beside him on the couch just as he had done when she was a child terrified of thunderstorms. He knew. They had been too close for too many years for him not to.

Whether Marla and Carl believed her contrived story for leaving town was debatable. More than likely they were so relieved by her absence they didn't want to delve too deeply.

As for the rest of the townspeople—well, they could think what they wanted. Amanda's softly drawn lips tightened in the delicate oval of her face. At least here she wouldn't have to listen to them or try to avoid them.

She gave her head a willful toss, making the short blond cluster of curls bounce in reaction. If she had learned nothing else from this experience, it was that she had reserves of strength she had never before known she possessed. She still loved Carl—she probably always would—but she would make a life without him. Modesty not withstanding, she knew she was more than just a little talented in art. Possibly her uncle would be willing to coach her. And one thing was certain—the money she had saved over the years would take her a long way until she knew if she could make a living as an artist. If not, well, there were other banks. . . .

Feeling a slight degree better, Amanda allowed her gaze to focus on the land around her. She had never been to her uncle's ranch before, her father had always claimed to be too busy at the feed store he ran to make the trip. So everything was new to her and she found it beautiful in a wild, rugged sort of way. The soil was dry and rocky, supporting thin wisps of needlelike grass. Trees stood in scrubby clumps in the hot brilliance of the midday sun, and the ribbon of road ahead twisted as far as the eye could see—up, down, and around the rolling hills. But it was the twin brick pillars standing like sentinels on either side of a narrow drive that at last reclaimed Amanda's attention. They were painted white and on their rough surface was the name, THE DOUBLE L, proudly lettered in black wrought iron. Her uncle's ranch.

Amanda took a deep bracing breath and restarted the engine of her car. The clatter of a metal cattle guard announced her entrance.

She had to travel some distance before a rambling old ranch house built of native white limestone came into view. The house was long and low with a porch running the length of the front. To one side a windmill turned in easy companionship to the slight breeze and at the rear a number of outbuildings were scattered about. Red-brown groups of white-faced cattle were huddled under scatterings of trees, taking advantage of what little shade they could find—her uncle's Herefords, his pride and joy next to his paintings.

Amanda brought her dusty red Volkswagen to a halt in front of the house. Then, after taking yet another deep breath, she opened the door and slid her feet to the hard surface of the ground. Her legs were a little cramped from the long drive, so she was forced to take the two steps leading up to the porch stiffly. The large front door was solid to her touch as she knocked.

While she waited she looked about appreciatively, noting the trio of chairs placed invitingly on the porch's wooden flooring and the large hanging basket that had a profusion of red and pink flowers cascading over its side. It was only after a time, when there was no answer, that she knocked again but with the result the same—no response. A slight frown began to wrinkle Amanda's smooth brow. She knew her uncle wasn't here, but Mrs. Gowen or the foreman should be. They knew she was coming today. Her frown became more pronounced as she walked

13

around the back of the house and tried the door there but as before gained no better results.

Hot, tired, and more than a little thirsty from the long trip from Kemperville to Craigmont, Amanda began to chew her bottom lip. What should she do now? Her jeans felt sticky as they clung to her legs, and her thin cotton blouse, which had started the day in crisp freshness, was now feeling as if she had worn it a week instead of just a day.

While wondering what her next move should be, her eyes settled on the scattering of outbuildings, and she gave a relieved sigh. That was where everyone would be! This was a working ranch, and just because she was expected today, the people her uncle employed wouldn't be lined up waiting to receive her. They would be working! With a renewed spring of confidence to her step Amanda pushed her way through the gate of the low white fence that separated the house yard from the outer ranch grounds. If necessary, she would go to each building. Surely she would find someone.

But ten minutes later Amanda was still searching. She had checked the barn and what must have been an equipment shed, disturbed a flock of chickens in their house, and come upon several horses in a corral. But she had yet to come in contact with another human being. And there was only one place left to look. She had kept it as a last resort. If no one was there, the ranch was deserted. Fighting down a sense of rising irritation, Amanda mounted the large flagstone step set before the building that could either be a bunkhouse or an office. She hesitated only a second before rapping on the heavy wooden door. If willpower alone could make another person appear, then someone definitely would come. But still there was no response.

Annoyed, Amanda knocked again, hoping and yet

14

knowing that it would do no good. Immediately she turned on her heel, narrowed her tawny gaze against the glare, and made a megaphone of her hands. "Mrs. Gowen! Boyd!" she called.

Still nothing moved; only the far off lowing of a calf broke the hovering stillness. She tried again, only louder. *"Mrs. Gowen! Boyd!"* Unease was beginning to replace irritation. Where was everyone? *"Mrs . . ."*

Her voice came to a strangled halt in her throat and all the blood seemed to rush from her body as the heavy weight of a hand shot out from behind and descended roughly on her shoulder, encasing her in frozen immobility.

A deep drawling masculine voice followed, requesting huskily, "Lady, would you please stop all that yelling? I've got one hell of a headache, and you're not doing it one damn bit of good."

The words seemed the key to Amanda's paralysis. She jerked about, causing the grip on her shoulder to be released.

Her heart was pounding from fright, but it gave another startled leap when her eyes traveled the long distance up the man's lean muscular form to look into his face. If a film company wanted to cast the part of a hardened ruffian, she had just found the perfect specimen.

Amanda stared blankly at him; then as the hand that had rested on her shoulder slowly moved until it was supporting a great part of the man's weight on the doorframe, his words registered in her brain, and she realized just what kind of headache he was complaining of. It was a hangover! His narrowed gray eyes were bloodshot and bleary-looking; the stubble of dark beard on his strong jaw was obviously more than a day's growth; his dark hair was unkempt, falling over his forehead and curling over the edge of the collar of his rumpled plaid shirt; his dirty jeans fitted as if they were a part of him.

15

Amanda's small straight nose twitched with distaste. "Well, I'm not exactly standing out here in the hot sun for my health either!" she snapped, her golden eyes flashing with immediate resentment. She had had enough trouble from the male branch of the species lately and she wasn't about to let this one get away with anything—especially when he was still very much the worse for drink!

The man shifted position, wincing at her still-raised voice. "Look, lady, I don't—"

"*I* am Amanda," she interrupted icily. If he were Boyd, the foreman, the name should manage to pervade his drunken haze.

The man sighed impatiently. "I don't give one red cent in hell *who* you are—" he began before his deep husky voice ground the sentence to a halt. He then repeated her name slowly to himself, as if trying to clear the fog in his head.

Amanda's temper overflowed. Obviously, since her uncle had been away for the last few days, the foreman had decided that this was a perfect opportunity to go on an uninterrupted drinking spree, forgetting in his stupor that she was scheduled to arrive.

"Yes. Amanda Reynolds, John Reynolds's niece." She paused to look him over in undisguised disapproval. "The one you were supposed to look after, Boyd. But from the way things are now, it will have to be the other way around, won't it? Do you always drink yourself blind when my uncle leaves the ranch?"

The man's features became suddenly still at the unexpectedness of her attack; then, as the insult of her words penetrated fully, a swift angry flash of gray lightning coursed over the lissomeness of her body, taking in her slim shapely legs, trim hips, narrow waist, and the softly rounded swell of each breast as it pressed against the thin

16

material of her snug-fitting blouse. After what seemed an age, his gaze lifted to her eyes.

It took all of Amanda's concentration right then just to breathe, that devastatingly masculine look producing a chill of reactive fear like none she had ever experienced before. But almost as quickly as the look appeared, it vanished. The man's stiffly held body was relaxed and indolent, and his expression was one of hazy indifference. Amanda was left to wonder if the metamorphosis had occurred.

Trying to reassure herself, she gave him another searching glance and decided that he was harmless enough. She had seen his type before in her work at the bank. They came into town, taking odd jobs at the surrounding farms —good workers until they got a little money in their pockets. How in the world a man of this type had become her uncle's foreman, she didn't know. But then, remembering the tales her father had told about his older brother as a child, bringing all the strays in the area home for care, she thought she understood a little better. Maybe he felt sorry for this man, sensing in him something she didn't. Maybe he was trying to help him—give him responsibilities. Not that it seemed to be doing much good.

Feeling a little ashamed—she never enjoyed losing her temper—Amanda forced herself to apologize. "Look," she said, trying to give a convincing little laugh, "I'm sorry. I'm hot; I'm tired. I've been driving for three and a half solid hours and I need to rest. Then I find that I can't get into the house, and there's no one around to let me in." She chanced a quick glance to the bronzed face above, but it still remained carefully impassive. Swallowing a surge of returning anger—he seemed to be waiting for more!—she continued. "I don't really mean to judge you. What you do when my uncle is away is between the two of you. I—"

"Very nicely put. Thank you," he interrupted sardonically, straightening and casually tucking his thumbs into the front loops of his jeans.

Amanda's face flamed at the more than small hint of sarcasm in his words; then, thinking it might be politic to change the subject, she asked after the housekeeper.

"Is Mrs. Gowen here?"

"Nope," came the drawled reply, his eyes never leaving her face. It was as if he were memorizing her every freckle! Amanda was distinctly uncomfortable. She ran the tip of her tongue over her dry lips, moistening them before replying with an inadequate, "Oh!" She didn't know why, but a sudden feeling of panic was invading her very bones, and she had the insane desire to run as far as she could go, even back to Kemperville. She wished her uncle had been here or even Mrs. Gowen—anyone, so that she wouldn't have to deal with the person standing so imposingly in front of her. So hard and tough and masculine!

"Uh . . . if you have a key, I'll let myself in. Then you can go back to your, uh—" She had started to say drinking but decided not to. She didn't want to offend him any more than she already had. After all, he was her uncle's foreman.

But this time, instead of reacting adversely, a thread of humor came into his voice as he drawled casually, "Now, that's an idea."

Amanda averted her eyes in confusion, looking out over the rugged land that still had to be fought to be conquered. Were the people and the land the same here? she wondered. Tough, unyielding?

"The door's not locked, Miss Reynolds." The man interrupted her thoughts. "We very seldom lock a door around here. Now, if that's all you need, I'll go back to my—uh—" Her gaze was reclaimed as he motioned with his hand to the interior of the building. "When you get unpacked, come join me. I don't mind sharing."

Amanda's gold-flecked gaze was wide in the delicate oval of her face as she absorbed his remarkable offer. Then, on seeing the laughing mockery that was barely hidden in the silvery-gray depths of his eyes, her teeth came together with a decided snap.

"No, I don't believe I care to, Boyd. I get my pleasure from other sources," she answered stiffly, and could have kicked herself because she sounded so prim—so much like Aunt Margaret, who seemed to disapprove of everything that could in any way be thought of as fun.

The gray eyes were now dancing. "Oh, so do I, Miss Reynolds, so do I. Women play almost as important a role in my life as drink. What's that poem about wine, women, and song?" He paused as if trying to think of the words. "Can't remember it now." He shrugged lightly. "In any case, I've had the wine this morning—or rather whiskey— and I remember humming something earlier, but I haven't had a woman yet today—" Amanda took a short step backward, away from the door, but in spite of her instinct warning her that she should not, she couldn't help the fascinated way she was regarding him. "So, if you don't want that old saying to come true, you'd better stop standing there giving me ideas. My bed's a single, but two can fit into it with very little trouble and with quite a degree of interest."

Murmuring a protest woven both with outrage and apprehension, Amanda turned to run the long distance back to the house, not pausing until she was safely through the picket fence and inside the back door—its firmness giving reassurance to her back as she leaned against it in relief.

Horrible man! she raged to herself, trembling all over as the echo of his laughter, which had followed her flight across the yard, still rang in her ears. Oh, how she hated

19

him! He was everything she disliked in a man: big, tough, challenging—immoral. He was nothing like Carl—nothing!

Cautiously she bent to chance a quick peek through the curtains of the window at one side of the kitchen door. The door to the bunkhouse was closed now; there was no sign of the man's disturbing presence.

Amanda immediately wrenched herself upright. Now why had she thought that? And why had she unconsciously given the word a sexual connotation? He wasn't disturbing. He was crude, dirty, and much worse the wear from drink. How could she possibly think of him as being disturbing? There was nothing attractive about him except a certain amount of rugged good looks, which the whiskey he boasted of would soon dissipate. He looked to be in his mid-thirties. It probably wouldn't be long before the bronze of his face became sallow and the whipcord muscles of his lean hard body became weak.

Determinedly Amanda shook her head, forcing herself to attain some distance from the incident. It was such a waste; but what the foreman chose to do with his life wasn't her concern. She had enough problems to deal with. She couldn't add his to her burden as well. He would have to take care of his own troubles himself.

When her heartbeat finally returned to normal, Amanda pushed herself away from the door and began to look around the house that would be her home for the next few months. It didn't take long to find that the large comfortably furnished rooms exuded the same feeling of lived-in warmth she had found on the outside. And she concluded that at least as far as the housekeeper was concerned, her uncle had found a jewel. Everything was neat and tidy, and the old-style kitchen with its scattering of time-saving devices was spotless.

The only room that proved an exception was the area

her uncle used for painting—a converted bedroom that held a jumble of canvases, paints, assorted sketches, and, as she looked closely, a liberal sprinkling of dust—which made her decide humorously that Mrs. Gowen must have been ordered to give this room wide berth.

As she strolled farther in, her nose wrinkled in appreciation of the distinctive smells of turpentine and oils. Then, spotting some finished canvases stacked against one wall, Amanda paused to examine them. Her uncle was truly a talented man, she thought with awe as she went from one painting to another. She had seen samples of his work in magazines and newspapers and her father owned a beautiful painting of her mother that Uncle John had done years ago; but now, seeing a collection like this, she was hit with the tremendous energy they exuded. Her uncle seemed able to bring life to the subjects he painted—a vibrancy that attacked one's senses—whether it was a child lying disconsolately on a ghetto porch, or the strong wrinkled face of an old woman who had experienced the most life had to offer, or a working cowboy sitting exhausted on a tired horse at the end of a hard day.

With a sigh Amanda set the paintings back into place. Seeing the work of a master made her feel so inadequate—even if he was her uncle. Would she ever be even half as good?

Not a chance! she decided wistfully, with one last glance at the paintings. Then she brightened. Not everyone was a Renoir or a Remington. She would have to develop her own style. And from the number of compliments she had received on some of her work over the years, she definitely must have something.

Her high aspirations were soon brought back to the mundane by a loud protesting rumble from her stomach. Breakfast had been ages ago and she suddenly discovered that she was starving.

Rummaging in the refrigerator produced the remnants of a casserole needing only to be warmed, so while she waited Amanda munched her way through a cookie and let her mind drift, as it had many times before, to speculation as to why her father had never brought his family to visit his brother's ranch. His stated reason that he couldn't leave his business just didn't make sense any longer. They had friends, any number of whom would have been more than willing to help out. So why? Her only conclusion—and this came from intuition rather than fact—was that there had been some kind of argument between the two brothers. Not that it ever showed when her uncle visited them during his infrequent trips to Dallas to arrange for showings of his work. It was just that at certain times when her father spoke of John an air of regret would enter his voice and she would be left to wonder.

After washing the few dishes she had used, Amanda brought her suitcases in from her car and chose a bedroom, calling it her temporary home. The room had large windows, allowing a great deal of light to enter, and she happily judged it would do perfectly for her own ministudio. Then she located the bathroom and took a quick shower, emerging a short time later refreshed and ready to take up the challenge she had issued herself. Coming here might have started out as an excuse to get away from the wedding plans and from the sight of Carl and Marla together, but she wasn't going to allow it to continue that way. This was the beginning of a new life and she wasn't going to waste it. Seeing her uncle's paintings had rekindled her enthusiasm to create, and her fingers almost itched to put pencil to paper.

With that need fully in control, Amanda pushed her way through the gate at the back of the house. Momentarily she gave thought to the foreman, but dismissed it. He had probably continued with his drinking and was now totally oblivious to everything—even a full brass band playing the national anthem just outside his window. But all the same she found herself tiptoeing on the hard ground as she passed in front of the bunkhouse door. Just in case, she told herself, knowing that the less contact she had with the man the better. Her uncle was going to be back in a week or ten days, and in the meantime, Mrs. Gowen, when she returned from wherever she was, would provide a buffer so that she wouldn't have to see Boyd again—unless she wanted to, which was an unsettling thought in itself.

After several hours spent sitting in the shade of a clump of stunted oak trees, a pad of paper propped on her knees, making repeated studies of the house, with its weathered exterior, white picket fence, windmill, water cistern, and the rolling hills beyond, Amanda became conscious of an overwhelming tiredness. Her eyes were beginning to burn and blur, and her back was crying out for a comfortable bed.

A series of wide yawns later, during which she could barely continue to focus her eyes, she gave in to her body's need for rest and began to gather her materials. She had not been sleeping at all well lately, and after the events of the day, found she was exhausted. She would make an early night of it, going to bed now, regardless of the fact that dusk was only just beginning to descend. There was nothing to stay up for anyway, no one to care about what she did.

She brushed off the seat of her jeans and slowly made her way back to the house, the familiar sounds of a dog barking in the distance and a confused rooster crowing at the end of the day instead of the beginning causing her mouth to curve into a light smile. Some things are the same wherever you go, she thought, fighting off another yawn.

As she approached the bunkhouse, though, some of her sleepiness disappeared, to be replaced by the now-familiar unease. She gave a tentative look toward the door but finding it was still safely closed, exhaled a small sigh and continued her way to the main house. That she had hesitated, however, annoyed her. Why she should even think of the man was mystifying. He was nothing to her! Then perversely her mind skipped on to consider what he would be like sober and decently dressed. He could be an extremely handsome man if he tried. The strong line of his jaw; the firm well-shaped mouth; the high cheekbones, whose structure added character to his face; the straight-cut nose; those unusual silvery eyes . . . Yes, if he tried, he would be a man few women could forget, because even in his hungover state, there had been something about him—a kind of hard sensuality that appealed to the senses rather than the mind.

Impatiently Amanda fought down the remembrance, concentrating instead on how impossibly maddening the man could be. Mocking her. He hadn't truly meant it when he taunted her about taking her to his bed; he had just said it to get a reaction—which, much to her chagrin, he had gotten. She had acted like a skittish schoolgirl, running away as if the devil himself were attempting to usher her into hell. And he had laughed. But he wouldn't have that opportunity again. She would stay out of his way completely. She would occupy herself with the job at hand, and by the time her uncle returned, she would have a large portfolio of sketches to show him. And she wouldn't think about the foreman!

With her mind turned resolutely to other affairs, Amanda didn't notice that the back door she had earlier closed on her way out of the house was now partially ajar, and that the old-fashioned windup ceiling fan was turning slowly, gently circulating the warm air of the kitchen.

Unaware of any of this, Amanda turned to lock the door behind her. They didn't lock doors here, the man had said, but she would! She was a creature of habit to some degree, and this was one habit she could not bring herself to break. Kemperville was much too close to Dallas for the residents of the sleepy little town to ignore the practicalities of life, for their own safety. Safety! That was what she needed more than anything else at this moment: a refuge where she could recover from the shock delivered two weeks before, where she would not have to pretend, where she could ease some of her pain by immersing herself in her art.

Amanda rested her forehead against the smooth wood of the door for a moment before turning to put a kettle of water on the electric stove. She was tired, but her drowsiness had abated somewhat since walking by the bunkhouse. Something else to blame on the foreman, she thought unreasonably.

She reached into a cabinet for a cup and was in the act of placing it on the counter when an all-too-familiar voice broke into her thoughts and caused her to jump almost out of her skin.

"I'll take mine black," it said, a certain sense of dryness evident in the request, "if you have some extra."

Startled amber eyes were quickly directed to the long lean body of the foreman as he lounged in the living-room doorway. He still wore the same dirty jeans and crumpled shirt as before, but at least this time he had the appearance of having washed and shaved. His unruly dark hair was combed, and his eyes had a more alert look about them. With one part of her mind Amanda noted the improvements; but with another, she registered embarrassed anger at being surprised.

25

"What are you doing in here?" she demanded, glaring at him.

"Trying to find you, what else?" The slow drawl of his voice was exaggerated, as was the indolent stance of his body. A slow smile pulled at his lips.

"Well? You've found me. What do you want?"

Anger took a backseat to trepidation as his narrowed eyes swept from her curly head to her small narrow feet and back again, pausing appreciatively on the feminine curves her fresh jeans and T-shirt revealed.

Amanda's body tensed, ready to run if she had to, but her legs were strangely weak. She didn't know if she could get very far. She watched him warily, but he didn't move. He just kept looking at her, observing the range of emotions she knew her face was displaying.

When he at last spoke, his voice was soft. "I just came to see if you have everything you need. I believe I'm supposed to play host—or so you said earlier."

Amanda let out a long quivering breath. The man unnerved her, but he was her uncle's foreman, for God's sake—not some kind of psychotic rapist! She looked away, her eyes fastening onto the cup she still held in her hands. Her tone strove for lightness as she replied, "I've found everything I need, thank you. You don't have to concern yourself about me any longer. I'm going to have some coffee and go to bed, and when I wake up in the morning, Mrs. Gowen will be here, and everything will be fine." She knew she was going on like an idiot, but the words kept tumbling out as if she were trying to reassure herself more than him. Which she was!

Even with her eyes on the cup, Amanda was conscious of the man's movement as he straightened and moved farther into the room. She tried to keep her heart steady, but it was hopeless. The nearer he came, the more it fluttered. He didn't stop until he was standing directly across from her.

"That's where I think we're going to run into a little problem."

"What do you mean?" Amanda choked, turning her face up to his and finding that he was much closer than she thought. She could see the tiny network of lines at the corners of his eyes that many hours of work in the bright sun had permanently etched, and the harsher lines running down each cheek that deepened when he was amused.

He watched her closely, his eyes dwelling on her parted lips. Then he said, "I mean that Mrs. Gowen isn't going to be back tomorrow, or probably the next day either. She and . . . the man who was driving her into town had a little accident yesterday. Oh, it wasn't bad," he assured her, seeing her concern, "but they're both in the hospital, and I don't know when they'll be back."

For the second time that evening the only word Amanda could think of to say was "Oh." She had been counting so much on the housekeeper's return, and now it seemed she wasn't going to—at least not for some time to come.

"So," the man continued, "I guess that means it's up to me."

"W-what is? I mean, what do you mean?" Amanda breathed the questions naively. She was still trying to deal with her violent reaction to his nearness. She didn't understand what was happening to her!

"That it's up to me to look after you, of course. There's no one else." A dark eyebrow lifted. "Which bedroom did you choose?"

Amanda's heart jumped, and even the screaming of the teakettle did not fully divert her attention, even though her fingers automatically moved to the knob.

A large work-roughened hand reached out and, covering her own, helped turn the burner off then move the kettle over so that its piercing scream would stop.

"I'm asking because I want to know which room to use myself. You didn't think I expected you to let me share yours, did you?"

Amanda could not immediately answer. She stared at him as if mesmerized. But the cause was not so much the content of his words as the lingering sensation from the touch of his hand. Her emotions were catapulting about as if she had been touched by fire. What was happening to her? Oh, God! She loved Carl! She didn't even *like* this man! So why did she respond to him so wildly? She had known Carl for as long as she could remember, and his touch had never affected her this way. God, she had met this man only this very afternoon!

"Or would you?" The soft, huskily spoken inquiry jolted Amanda out of her shocked state.

"*No!* No, I . . ." she began to stutter.

"I didn't think so. Too bad." He lifted a shoulder then straightened to his full height. "You still didn't say which room is yours."

Taking refuge in anger, Amanda tried to ignore the jellylike feel of her knees. "That's right, I didn't! And I don't intend to. I'm not a child. I don't need you to baby-sit. I'm perfectly capable of taking care of myself."

The man was slowly shaking his dark head. "Nope. I'm staying. If Hazel were here, it would be different; but she's not, and I know John wouldn't want you left to fend for yourself."

Amanda felt like stamping her foot. "I am not a child!"

The silver eyes glinted meaningfully. "Lady, you don't have to tell me that."

Amanda struggled to stave off the flurry of excitement that was coursing through her body. All the man had to do was look at her!

"Is that supposed to make me feel better?" she blustered. "Somehow taking my chances with a group of Hell's Angels sounds better. And if my uncle truly knew you for what you are, he'd feel the same way too!"

The second the words were out she wished she'd never said them. It was one thing to think badly of someone and another to throw that fact in his face. The sudden stiffening of the man's body, the tight clamping of his jaw, and the polar iciness that entered his gray eyes as they held her own told of a barely restrained anger. Amanda cringed inwardly but refused to let it show.

"What are you afraid of, Miss Reynolds?" he asked bluntly, contempt giving an added edge to his words. "That if you spend the night in my bed a little of that prim frigid shell you call a body might melt and become more human? Who knows? You just might enjoy the experience."

Most of the color drained from Amanda's face only to come rushing back to flood it a brilliant scarlet. No one—no one—had ever talked to her in such a way before.

As he watched her indignant groping for words, a little of his anger seemed to dissipate and a degree of his previous condescending humor returned. "You don't have to worry though, honey. I won't bother you. I like my women warm and friendly, and in the past they haven't been all that hard to find."

Amanda swallowed convulsively, the insult tearing through her, making her want to retaliate. "No—I'm sure they haven't," she retorted caustically. "They probably fall all over you at the bars you visit."

For several breathless seconds Amanda thought he was going to hit her. His hands clenched into fists at his sides, his lazy smile disappeared, and his teeth almost gritted in anger.

"I think you'd best go to that bedroom of yours now,

29

Miss Reynolds. Because if you don't, I won't be responsible for what happens."

Amanda responded to his biting instruction with a willful toss of her head. She didn't feel very defiant inside, but she couldn't afford to let him know that.

He didn't move a muscle as she brushed past, wasting no time in crossing to the door. But once she was there she paused to give the man who so dominated the room one last look—drawn by the intensity of the pale gaze that had followed her every move.

Several long beats of time passed as Amanda wordlessly stared at him, then she turned and walked into the hall, her back straight, her chin held high, but with her emotions a chaotic tangle.

## CHAPTER TWO

The next morning the only evidence Amanda found of the foreman's presence in the house was his breakfast dishes, which were neatly stacked and drying in the dish drainer. Not having slept at all well, she glared at them, wishing by some chance that the inanimate dishes could convey her feelings to their previous user. Much of her night had been spent in composing crushing replies that would have cleverly put him in his place. But, as always, these brilliant ripostes seldom came when needed, and telling them to her pillow just was not quite the same thing as having the satisfaction of saying them to the man himself.

Amanda prepared her own breakfast—toast spread with a delicious peach preserve she found in the refrigerator—then decided to spend the morning further exploring the area around the house. Last evening she had been too tired to do more than find a convenient shady place and plop herself down to sketch the first thing at hand. But this morning she had a little more energy, and, anyway, she needed something to get her mind off recurring thoughts of the foreman.

It stood to reason then that seeing him the first thing upon leaving the house was obviously not a welcome occurrence. He was outside the barn talking to another man, who stood just inside the open door of a dark blue pickup.

Amanda started to waver in her course the instant she

saw him but was stopped by the challenging glance the foreman directed over her before turning his attention back to the other man. Provoked, she sent his handsome profile a fulminating look. She would be damned if she was going to let him think he could intimidate her again! Maybe last night he had—a little—but this was another day. She was going to play it cool and calm and she wasn't going to let him get the upper hand. And she wasn't going to let him confuse her! Armed with these new resolves, Amanda directed her steps toward the men.

The man the foreman was talking to proved to be wiry and short, not much taller than her own five foot two inches, with weathered skin, and bright, almost piercing black eyes. His glance seemed to sum her up in one look; he was introduced to her as Jake Farling.

Amanda smiled as pleasantly as she could during the introduction, conscious all the while of the foreman's presence, extending her small hand and saying she was pleased to meet another of her uncle's men. She was somewhat amused at the man's abrupt manner, as without saying a word he gave her hand a sturdy shake then let it go and nodded his head. His dark eyes were still fastened on her face, but with him she felt no sense of uneasiness. He was about the same age as the foreman, but there was an underlying shy friendliness about him that was reassuring.

"You look like you feel better this morning, Miss Reynolds. Did you sleep well?" The mocking tone in the familiar deep voice grated on Amanda's straining nerves.

"Well enough, thank you," she answered, darting a cool glance to the tall man by her side.

"That's good," he drawled. "Can't have you being upset by the change and all. Strange rooms and strange beds are a little lonely sometimes."

On one level his words seemed innocent enough, carefully stated so as not to pique the interest of the hired hand, yet on another, it was a direct dig at her, and she recognized it as such.

Her cheeks took on added color, but her reply was even as she answered, "I've never found that to be a problem before."

"No, I suppose not."

As his bland agreement intended for her to do, Amanda turned to look at him fully. His silver eyes captured hers and richly conveyed his unspoken words: that frigid little virgins seldom do.

It took all of Amanda's self-restraint not to slap him. Her golden eyes flashed fire, and she was almost trembling with fury as she fought the silent war with her will. Slowly she became aware of the fact that Jake Farling was shuffling uncomfortably in the sun. His gaze was firmly fixed on the ground as his fingers played absently with the door handle. He was a much more perceptive man than she had thought, and this verbal battle between his immediate boss and his employer's niece was making him uncomfortable —but then again, maybe he knew the foreman too well and had seen all this before.

Containing herself with difficulty, Amanda made her voice level as she forced a tight smile in the direction of the hired hand. "It was nice meeting you, Mr. Farling. I'm sure we'll see more of each other. Now, if you'll excuse me, I'm going for a walk."

She started to move away, pointedly ignoring the foreman's presence, but he wasn't content with that. He halted her with four well-chosen words: "Watch out for rattlers."

Amanda froze to the spot. If there was one thing she liked even less than thunderstorms, it was snakes. Horror shot through her at the thought of encountering a rattlesnake. She had known that the land around here abounded in them but had forgotten. Once when she was a child, Uncle John had brought her the tail of a rattler to play

33

with, and she had been fascinated with it until she learned its source. After that she had not even wanted to look at it. Amanda forced her petrified limbs to loosen. She couldn't let the foreman see the effect his words had had on her: he would enjoy the experience far too much. So jerkily, without turning, she answered stiffly, "Don't worry, I'll be careful."

She had started to walk away—on legs that felt curiously like two wooden pegs, when his parting shot made her ears burn.

"It's not you I'm worried about, honey, it's the snake. The poor thing won't stand a chance."

A low protesting murmur came from Jake, but it was soon drowned out by the foreman's hearty laughter.

Amanda quickened her pace and didn't stop until she was out of view over a small hill. Oh, how she hated that man! She hated him! If only she were a man, she would make him eat those words. She would beat him to within an inch of his life—he would be begging for mercy. A small sob rose in her throat and angry tears rushed into her eyes only to be blinked furiously away as she cursed herself for being so vulnerable.

Amanda remained outdoors for most of the morning, snakes of the reptilian variety holding little place in her thoughts. When hunger finally made her turn back, she cautiously paused on a hillside that overlooked the working pens and outbuildings across the way. Her care was rewarded by the sight of the foreman busily saddling a light brown horse. Not wanting to encounter him again so soon, Amanda waited as he mounted and rode off in a direction clearly different from that of her approach. She watched until his lean-muscled body, moving in graceful unison with the horse, could no longer be seen.

That afternoon Amanda could settle down to nothing. Restlessly she turned on the television set but could not become absorbed in game shows, so she turned it off. And one of her uncle's books, a murder mystery she thought might help pass time, was sorely lacking in suspense, which soon caused her to lose interest.

Twilight was approaching when she decided to place a call to her father and dialed the familiar number, knowing that he would still be at the store.

When he answered, his voice so familiar and loved, Amanda's throat tightened and a rush of intense loneliness all but swamped her.

"How are you doing, sweetheart?" Patrick Reynolds asked as soon as Amanda had identified herself.

"I'm fine, Daddy," she said huskily, holding the receiver close. "I didn't have any trouble on the trip down."

"Good, good. I didn't think you would." He paused as if settling himself more comfortably. "John not back yet?"

"No—not yet, not until sometime next week."

"Umm. Well, I guess that housekeeper of his is taking good care of you. From the way John talks about her, the place would collapse around his ears if she ever decided to retire."

Amanda swallowed. They were getting to the sticky part. "No, she's not here, Dad. She—she had an accident. Not a bad one, but she won't be back for a few days."

"Are you there by yourself then?" Amanda heard the quick frown in her father's voice.

"Uh . . . no. The foreman's around," she answered vaguely. "And some of the other men." Not for a moment was she going to tell him that the foreman insisted on living in the house with her. Her father was a bit old-fashioned when it came to matters like that, and there would be no way in the world she could make him understand.

"Oh, Boyd." His relief was evident over the miles. "Never met him myself, but John always speaks highly of him. Had some trouble with the law a few years back, I believe, but he's been straight as an arrow ever since." Then, as if sensing the start his words had given, he tried to reassure her. "If John didn't think he could trust him, he wouldn't leave the ranch in his hands. So don't worry, sweetheart, Boyd will take care of you."

"That's what I'm afraid of," Amanda murmured to herself, not really meaning to say the words out loud, then had to hurry to invent something when her father asked what he had missed. "I said, I'm not afraid," she fabricated.

"Good. Umm—" Her father seemed hesitant to bring up the next subject. "Things are kind of hurrying along here. Marla and Carl have set a date. The middle of next month."

Amanda's heart took a plunge. "So soon?" she whispered. This was the first time she had thought about Carl today—and that was in itself a jolt—but to hear that the wedding was to take place so soon . . . It was good that she had come away.

"Carl wants everything settled before he has to start harvesting the grain sorghum." Her father paused as if not wanting to hurt her more than he already had. "They're taking a two-week trip to New Orleans for their honeymoon. A present from Carl's parents."

Amanda had to swallow hard to stem a sudden rush of tears, but sincerity rang in her voice as she all but whispered, "I hope they'll be happy, Dad. I really do." And she did. She really did. She loved both of them—no matter what they had done to her. And they probably had no accurate idea of how much she had been hurt. Amanda had to give herself credit for one thing—she was able to play a role convincingly, for a little time at least. When she had last seen them, they were as happy as two people

36

could be. That was what hurt so much—and seemed so unfair.

"I know you do, Andy. And I know that right now you think your world has come to an end. But it hasn't. Carl's not the right man for you, never has been. I've always known that. Now it will be up to you to find it out for yourself."

Amanda's sniff was audible over the long-distance line.

"Come on, pumpkin, give us a smile." Her father's old time-proved remedy for all her hurts when she was small had never failed to work, and this time was no different. Only now both of them knew the wound was not so shallow.

"Thanks, Dad." The tears in her golden eyes refused to be denied and slowly began to fall down over her cheeks. But for her father's sake she had to end the conversation on a positive note. He was worried enough about her already. So with a bravado that was completely hollow she retorted gamely, "Maybe Boyd will be the one to show me Carl was just a—a dream. He's not too bad to look at . . ." *And willing,* she added to herself, as she tried to rub the traces of her tears away.

Her father's answering hoot of laughter made her frown down at the hall table in puzzlement. "From what John's said, he's as ugly as sin and about thirty years too old for you. But don't let that stop you, Andy. Sometimes life's best prizes come in slightly dilapidated packages. Well, I've got to go. There's a delivery of fertilizer that's come up missing. Remember that I love you and tell John hello for me when you see him."

"I will, Dad," she promised, and was still frowning, mystified, as she slowly replaced the receiver on it's cradle. Boyd? Ugly? And old? He wasn't *that* old. And he certainly wasn't ugly—not by any stretch of the imagination. Dissipated, maybe, when he had been drinking for long

37

periods of time. Hateful, maddening. But that wasn't what her father had said. Maybe he had Boyd confused with someone else. Uncle John was always telling them stories about the interesting people he met. Yes, that must be it. Boyd wasn't the man her father was talking about.

Then the memory of what her father had told her about the approaching wedding put all other thoughts from her mind. Oh, God! A little over a month! How was she ever going to get through the wedding? She couldn't possibly not go. The gossips would really have a field day then. And, knowing Marla, with the success of her deception making her sister think that everything was fine, she would probably want her to be in the wedding party.

With a groan Amanda threw herself facedown onto the sofa and gave in to her need to cry. She would have to go; she would have to force herself to stand there with a smile on her face and watch her younger sister marry the man she had always thought to take as her husband. It was too much, it was just too much. The tears were flowing freely as she let the wound be torn open once again. She cried because she felt abused and battered and more than a little sorry for herself.

A short time later, with her face mottled from her orgy of tears, Amanda turned over onto her back and stared at the ceiling, not really seeing it or anything else. Her eyes were turned inward, going over the times when she and Carl had played as children, the first fumbling kiss he had planted on her lips at a school dance, the warm feeling she had always experienced at being known as his girl . . .

Suddenly a voice broke into her reverie. "I wondered when you'd decide to stop. What's the matter? Miss me?"

Nothing could have been guaranteed more to dry up her tears than those words—from the man she was fiercely growing to hate.

Amanda jackknifed into a sitting position and jerkily wiped her cheeks. She turned an outraged expression toward him as he leaned lazily against the doorframe. "No," she replied acidly, "I wouldn't miss you if you were the proverbial last man on earth."

For an answer he smiled slowly, a knowing, tantalizing smile that made Amanda seethe. Then he said, "You shouldn't let yourself be such an easy mark. You make much too tempting a target."

Reminded of his parting words about the snake and her hurried flight away, Amanda gritted her teeth and shot back, "And you shouldn't come into a room without making sure that you're welcome!"

She glared at him, but his smile only widened, deepening the attractive creases along either side of his tanned cheeks. "I haven't been welcome since the first time you set eyes on me, have I?"

Amanda raised her chin, not liking the taunting laughter behind his words. It was as if he was appreciating a secret joke—and the joke was on her!

"No." She was brutally honest.

"So I should be used to your rudeness by now."

Amanda's cheeks flushed, and she held her hands tightly together, making fists of them in her lap. Maybe if she refused to answer him, he would go away. She turned to look pointedly out the window.

He continued, unaffected by her seeming withdrawal. "Well, I'm not—but I guess I'll have to get used to it. I'd do anything for John Reynolds, even if it means putting up with his spoiled little niece."

Amanda gave the foreman a look of pure hatred. How dare he call her spoiled! He didn't know anything about her. And of all people, he was in no position to call anyone anything. She was just about to tell him so when he laughed shortly and began to turn away. "I'm going to take a shower. Why don't you see what you can rustle up for my supper? I haven't had time to eat anything since breakfast." It was more of a command than a request, and Amanda shot to her feet in an instant.

"Why you arrogant . . . ignorant . . . *cowboy!*" she spat. His calm assumption that she would do his bidding was more than she could stand. "Where does it read that *I* have to cook for *you*?"

Her angry question stopped his outward movement. She felt his silver eyes slide over her stormy face and move down over her trembling slenderness.

"I guess somewhere in the same pages that destined you to be a woman," he drawled easily.

"Oh!" Amanda stamped her small foot. To top everything off he was one of *that* kind of men. She should have known. A woman's place is in the home; keep her barefoot and pregnant! That was what he thought. Pity his poor wife—if he had one, which she seriously doubted. Who would be willing to put up with him? Amanda had never listened with much attention to the cry of the Women's Movement—neither her father nor Carl ever giving her cause—but now she wished she had.

"Aren't you being just a little archaic, Boyd?" Her words were sickeningly sweet as she tried with all her might to keep rein on her temper. "Most men stopped thinking that way years ago."

The foreman nodded, a glint in his pale eyes as he watched her struggle. "Maybe."

Amanda stared back at him, abstractedly noting the manner in which his dirt-streaked checkered shirt fitted across his muscular chest and shoulders; the way his sleeves were rolled back to the elbows, exposing his strong forearms; and the way fine dark hairs grew on his arms and sprinkled to a stop a little below his wrists on the back of his hands. An uncontrollable shiver ran down her spine.

In spite of herself and the temper that was simmering beneath the surface, she was drawn to him, and it frightened her.

Amanda swallowed, trying to call back her blazing anger, but uneasily found that she couldn't.

"What if I can't cook?" she asked at last.

The creases reappeared in his cheeks. "Honey, you don't look as if you've exactly starved today. I'll eat whatever you did."

The condescending sound of those words did the trick. Amanda's anger flared, and as a plan took shape in her head, she warned, "My tastes are a little . . . exotic. Maybe you won't like what I make."

"I'm easy to please. In most things a little extra spice never hurts."

Amanda just barely stopped herself from snapping at the bait. Her hand was itching to slap his handsome smiling face, but she remained still. She watched as he inclined his head in a short approving nod and turned away to disappear down the hall.

Oh! He had to be the most exasperating man on the face of the earth! And she had the honor of being stuck with him, at least for the next few days. If only he wasn't so damned attractive. And knew it! And knew that she knew it, which made it worse. A man as attractive as he probably had been seducing women from the time he was in the cradle. He probably thought he knew all about women. Well, this was one woman he would be surprised by. She wasn't going to roll over and play dead the instant he snapped his fingers. She wasn't even going to sit up— not unless it served a purpose she was intent upon.

A strong baritone voice singing a recent country hit above the sound of running water was enough to send Amanda hurrying on her way, a small wicked smile tilting

41

up the corners of her mouth. Let him sing—now. He wasn't going to have voice enough left to do so later.

The scrambled eggs Amanda had waiting on a plate looked innocent enough, if you discounted their slightly reddish cast. But she hoped that the foreman would be too hungry to notice—at least, until he tasted his first bite. She had set the table with care, using some of the better dishes she found stacked on a top shelf, arranging the silverware just so, even going so far as to venture out into the newly fallen night to gather a few of the daisies growing at the side of the house, arranging them attractively in a vase. Their white-and-yellow colors lent a festive air to the table, and Amanda had to smother an anticipatory smile as she heard his approach.

When he came into the room wearing a clean pair of jeans and snapping the lowest snap of a fresh cream-colored shirt, Amanda only raised an eyebrow. His hair was neatly combed but still damp from his shower and curled a little more than usual on the ends, and he had taken the time to shave. All these things Amanda saw, but she was too intent on what was going to happen in the next few moments to dwell upon them.

"Would you like some coffee?" Had her voice given her away?

The foreman frowned slightly, as if puzzled that she had sounded so friendly, but after a moment shrugged. "Sure, if you have some going."

"Of course." Amanda turned her back to pour the cup. It took much longer than she expected and for a time she despaired that she would have to spoon it out.

"Want to keep me company?" His invitation made her jump guiltily.

"No—no, thank you. I just ate."

42

He moved to the table and mounted the wooden chair as if it were a horse. "Looks pretty good."

Amanda's fingers twined into each other and it was all she could do not to jump up and down in glee as he took his fork and raised the first bite to his mouth.

But to her consternation he put it back down on the plate. "Forgot to salt it. Do you have any around?" He was watching her agitated state closely.

"I'll get it," she volunteered almost too quickly as she hurried across to the cabinet and returned with the salt shaker.

"Thanks," he answered gravely as she handed it to him. He shook out the white granules before slowly reclaiming his fork.

Amanda watched in frozen fascination as he chewed the first bite without blinking an eye. Then, as he reached for another, her eyes widened until they became as large as saucers.

With each successive bite her agitation increased, until she was almost wringing her hands. Didn't he feel it? God, she had put enough hot sauce in the eggs to burn even the most faithful jalapeño-pepper fanatic's mouth! How could he just sit there and eat it so calmly?

"Pretty good" was his slight praise when he had finished. Was it just her imagination that his eyes looked a little glassy and that his voice was a shade higher than before? But if it had affected him adversely, he was doing an excellent job of hiding it.

"Want to put a little milk in that coffee?"

Like a rabbit fascinated by a snake, Amanda moved to do as he asked. She watched with growing horror as he began to stir the liquid. When the cup was almost to his mouth, she could stand it no longer.

"Don't!" she cried.

He raised his eyebrows in mute question.

"Don't drink that!" She rushed to the table and tried to take the cup from his hands, suddenly ashamed of what she had done. All he had asked was that she fix him a meal. Was she so poor-spirited that she couldn't do even that? He had worked hard all day; she could tell by the state of his dirt-encrusted clothing and the tired way he had massaged his neck as he had watched her from the doorway. All she had done all day was sit. Was preparing a meal really too much to ask? "Please," she pleaded, her golden eyes filled with regret.

"Why?"

"You know why." She succeeded in taking the cup from his unresisting hand. "Why did you—I mean, why did you do it?"

"I told you I don't mind a little spice, and if you were a little heavy-handed—"

"A little?" she interrupted incredulously. "I used an entire bottle of hot sauce!"

The foreman swallowed tightly before getting to his feet. "I wondered how much you'd used. God, woman! Get me some water!"

Through a haze of tears Amanda saw the smile that flashed on his face and the even white teeth it exposed. A nervous laugh escaped as she ran to the sink and started filling a glass. Impatient hands took it from her.

A number of glasses later, both Amanda and the foreman began to laugh, quietly at first, then with more enthusiasm. Finally, when they could contain themselves, Amanda collapsed in a chair at the table and the foreman followed suit, taking up a potholder and fanning himself.

"Were you trying to kill me or just prove that you don't like me?"

"A little of both, I think," Amanda answered honestly, coming as close to liking him as she ever had before.

"You almost succeeded." Silver eyes smiled into her

44

own, then went over her delicately featured face with its small straight nose, soft mouth, and mop of curly blond hair. "Looks like an angel and acts like a—"

"Never mind. Don't say it. I know." She raised a hand in the air to stop him. "How in the world did you eat those eggs?"

"I've been known to indulge in a few hot-pepper eating contests in my life. I've never won, but after today I think I just might be able to."

Amanda looked down at her hands, suddenly unable to face him any longer. "I'm sorry," she apologized.

After a long minute a finger tipped her chin. She allowed her head to be raised but still refused to look at him.

"Forget it. I guess maybe I asked for it," he replied softly.

Amanda's gaze flickered up, and for the first time she really noticed the improvement in his appearance. He was just as she had imagined he would be, she thought bemusedly—strong, virile, and undeniably attractive— only now seeing the lines of good humor that softened his face, where before his taut expression had hidden them from view. Oh, he had laughed at her, taunted her, but that was not the same. Now, relaxed and sharing the laughter with her, he was very different. She began mentally to sketch his strong handsome features. She had never attempted to do a portrait before, landscapes being her natural bent, but with his face, she wondered if she couldn't be successful.

Time passed, and Amanda forgot that she was still staring at him. She only came to awareness when the sudden, strained silence of the room finally pierced her concentration. She had been studying his mouth, firm in its set, yet with a hint of sensuality to the fuller lower lip, when her eyes were drawn inexorably up to his. He was watching her intently, his gaze fixed firmly on her own lips; and when she moved slightly, nervously running the tip of her tongue over their curving softness, the expression in his eyes darkened and became even more intent. Slowly, as if against his will, he pulled his gaze away until he was looking directly into her eyes. What she saw in them made Amanda's heart begin to pound—whether from excitement or fear, she didn't know. A funny weightlessness began to affect her body.

"You better quit looking at me like that, honey," His voice was soft and slightly husky, but the warning he gave was deadly serious. "That is, if you still want me to keep to my own room tonight."

It was funny how situations could change in an instant. She had almost liked him for a time. But now the words he spoke pricked the bubble of tentative friendship with an abrasive finality. He wasn't the kind of man a woman could be merely friends with. To him, closeness between the sexes meant only one thing—sex.

To cover her embarrassment Amanda replied stiffly, "You're mistaken, Boyd. I wasn't looking at you in any special way." She had always heard that when you were dealt a losing hand in poker, you should bluff.

"The hell you weren't." He called her bluff.

Abruptly Amanda got to her feet, pushing her chair back in a single motion. She began to gather up the dishes. Now—if she remembered correctly—the better part of valor was discretion, so she retreated to the sink. "Have it your way. I couldn't care less what you think."

But instead of leaving, as she fully expected him to, he remained where he was, indolently lighting a cigarette as if nothing were wrong—as if they were enjoying the end of a quiet, peaceful evening.

In the distance thunder rumbled ominously, and Amanda couldn't control the tremor in her limbs as she moved to get the skillet from the stove. It was the coming storm that was causing this annoying weakness, she kept telling herself, not those silver eyes she could feel boring into her back. It was the storm!

She had been afraid of storms ever since the night her mother died and she had run out of the house to hide in a wooden lean-to that had long before been a favorite place to play. A terrible storm had passed over Kemperville that night, and it was not until several hours later that her father had found her huddled in a dark corner of the rickety building holding on to her favorite doll and whimpering in fright. The lightning and thunder had seemed more than frightening to her seven-year-old self— it had been terrifying. And the experience had remained with her, a dread reality in her subconscious.

"Looks like a bad one," the hateful voice commented from beside her.

She turned to find that he was standing at the window by the door. A shaft of lightning lighted up the darkness outside and soon was followed by a louder crash of thunder. Amanda's face whitened, and it was all she could do not to drop the skillet into the soapy water. Desperately she fought for control. She could not lose face in front of this man, she simply could not. If he was able to burn his mouth by eating her doctored eggs and not blink an eye, she could live through a storm. Any kind of storm. She straightened her shoulders and gritted her teeth, bracing herself for what was to come.

But Amanda's bravery was not destined to last long. She had just finished the dishes by exercising steel control, when much to her relief, the foreman decided to go outside to check on things. It was good to be alone—at first. She didn't have to hide each flinch as the cacophony of thunder was accompanied by yet another flash of lightning, but it soon became less of an advantage. The minutes seemed to drag.

Amanda lowered herself weakly to a chair, shutting her eyes tightly and covering her ears like a child as the storm's approach came nearer. She wanted to go to her room but couldn't make herself move. Brilliant white flashes alternated with reverberating crashes, and she sank farther and farther into the chair.

Ten minutes later she was still alone, and by this time she would have been glad to see Frankenstein's monster if he had been willing to hold her hand, so the arrival of the foreman was more than welcome.

His rain-slickered figure came through the door, and small rivulets of water ran onto the floor. Hurriedly she got to her feet to help him remove the heavy yellow covering.

"Don't know if we're going to get enough rain out of this to do any good, but I guess anything will help. What we need is a good all-day soaking and less show." He took the slicker from her hands and saw for the first time her whitened face and wide terror-filled eyes.

Amanda found that it was all she could do not to throw herself into his arms and beg to be held until the storm was over. But being held in her father's arms was something totally different from being held by this man. If she came to him for protection and comfort, he might get the wrong idea. Shakily she held herself back.

"You afraid of storms?"

He was asking the obvious, but Amanda nodded her head at the warm softness in his voice, her blond curls the most lively thing about her at the moment. The rest of her body felt frozen.

A white flash of brilliance that was so close it seemed to fill the room was followed instantly by a deafening clap of thunder. It had Amanda crying out and flying into the answering outflung arms. Nothing mattered to her now but the safety of another human body. Her eyes were tightly shut, and her cheek rested against the cream-colored shirt that covered his hard muscular chest. She felt the comforting hand at the small of her back and the other pressing her head close. She could hear a slow steady heartbeat and knew it was not her own. When she pried her eyes open, she found herself in a world of darkness.

The man felt the tremor that passed through her body and tried to comfort her. "Lightning struck close by. Must have knocked out a transformer." His voice seemed to come from a long distance away, but she could feel the rumble in his chest.

Amanda nodded in agreement but kept her arms tightly locked around him. She didn't want his warmth to go away.

After another moment she felt him move, and a strong hand came around to gently push her away. She resisted and was instantly folded back into his embrace.

Another flash lighted up the room. "Look," he suggested, "don't you think it would be a good idea to sit down or something?"

Amanda heard the humor that tinged his words and relaxed slightly. "I—I can't see anything." Her voice was small; she sounded lost.

"Neither can I. But if you'd let go for a minute, I can try to find a lantern or a flashlight—maybe even a candle."

Slowly Amanda released her hold, feeling suddenly cold as he moved away. "You won't have to go back outside, will you?" she asked tremulously, unconcerned at the vulnerability her words revealed.

"No. John should have something in the house."

She stood still as a match flicked into life and he began to search the kitchen cabinets. A grunt of satisfaction told her of his success; a moment later a warm yellow glow filled the room, making her blink in its brightness.

When she saw that the foreman was watching her,

49

Amanda looked away, embarrassed. She could think of nothing to say, so she held tightly to the back of the chair where he had left her.

"You don't look like you can take much more. Come on. Show me which room is yours, and I'll take you there."

He was holding out one hand and had a kerosene lantern in the other. Amanda slowly put her small cold fingers into his. The answering firm clasp did much to reassure her.

The storm seemed to be moving away as they made their way down the long hall to the bedroom. Only occasional flashes and softened rumbles told of its former fury.

Amanda was still trembling, but now she wasn't so sure of its source. The hard work-roughened hand holding her own was beginning to summon up feelings other than reassurance, as she remembered how it was to be held in those strong arms, as she recalled the heady masculine scent she had been too frightened at the time to respond to, the feel of his breath against her ear as he had brought his head protectively down to shield hers . . . it was all coming back.

When the door to her room was opened, Amanda hurriedly disengaged her hand and went inside. Then she nervously began to look around, feeling more than ever like a fool as the silence between them seemed to go on forever. She caught his gaze and looked at him blankly as he waited with the lantern still in his hand.

"Well?" His question caused her to jump.

"Well what?" she repeated breathlessly.

"Are you going to stand there all night? Get your things off and get into bed."

When Amanda just continued to look at him, the foreman uttered a muffled curse, put the lantern on a tall chest of drawers, and came to stand close in front of her.

50

"If you aren't the most exasperating female it's ever been my misfortune to meet," he began as his hands reached out to turn her around.

When she felt the bottom of her T-shirt begin to rise, Amanda gave a small protesting squeak; but it all came to naught. Before the sound fully left her lips, the shirt was being pulled unceremoniously over her head, and two strong hands were coming around to undo the snap of her jeans.

Amanda began to struggle, but only succeeded in bringing her body closer to the foreman's, feeling the heat of his chest burn into her naked back like a brand.

"Stay still, honey. I'm not going to hurt you." The impatience in his voice was muffled as he tried to still Amanda's twisting movement.

Whatever she did seemed to make the situation worse. All she wanted to do was get away. This forced intimacy was doing things to her that she had never experienced before.

"Let me go!" she yelped.

"Stop acting like a wildcat! All I'm trying to do is help you get into that damn bed. You didn't look like you were capable of doing anything for yourself a few minutes ago."

"Let—"

"Damn!"

In her fright Amanda had somehow hooked a foot around the foreman's leg. As she turned to protest the brush of his hand against the scanty scrap of lace that covered a breast, they lost their balance and fell on the bed. Amanda suffered the weight of his body as it crashed down on top of her.

After a stunned second she began to push frantically against the wall of his chest only to find her hands summarily gathered together and raised above her head, there to be held tightly by his.

51

Wild golden eyes stared up into the hard face above. Both of them were breathing hard from their efforts, and their legs were entangled as their feet still dragged on the floor.

Annoyance was creasing the foreman's brow; but slowly, as his gaze took in the delicate features of the face on the bed beneath him—the huge tawny eyes, the soft lips that were trembling in reaction, and lower, the desirable fullness of her partially exposed breasts—his eyes darkened and he murmured huskily, "Honey, I didn't plan it this way, but I'm only human . . ."

Amanda watched as his head lowered and his lips took possession of her own. At first she was too surprised to protest, then as his mouth began a slow sensual assault which was designed to stimulate her senses while at the same time add fuel to his mounting passion, all thought of protest vanished. A scorching flame was igniting deep in her body and mindlessly she capitulated to its burning insistence.

Nothing had ever prepared Amanda for the emotional tumult that followed. It was as if every molecule in her body had just been waiting for his touch, as if all the kisses she and Carl had exchanged were just a practice—a prelude—for what was to come.

The kiss deepened and Amanda's lips parted, allowing the moistness in his mouth to mingle intimately with hers. Her arms were released from their bondage, and as if unaware of their earlier struggle, wound about his neck to pull him even closer. His hands began to stroke the length of her body—exploring each curve with fresh discovery. Amanda moaned softly in response, entrapped by an aching tension that was increasing with each passing second.

His body was like a drug to her—the closer he came, the more contact she needed. Gone from her mind was any thought of Carl, any thought that this was a man she had just met—and whom she didn't even like. In her emotionally charged state, she didn't care.

His breathing was ragged when he raised his head to look at her. Amanda saw the naked desire in his eyes, but instead of being repelled, she was deeply excited. He began to trail kisses along the side of her neck and across the hollow of her throat, at the same time drawing aside the strap of her bra. Responding only to sensation, Amanda arched her body in pleasure, her breath catching as his mouth moved over the curve of one swelling breast to gently tease the hardened nipple. Amanda felt as if she were drowning in blissful oblivion.

Involved as the two of them were in mutual sensual enjoyment, the far-off ringing of the telephone was not assimilated for several long minutes, the sound being only a nagging irritation. Then the foreman's hand rested motionless on the curve of her hip and Amanda became still as the insistent sound permeated their consciousness.

Glittering silver eyes ran hungrily over her breasts and face before narrowing as he lowered his head for one final hard kiss on her responsive lips. Then, pushing away, he levered himself up from the bed and, taking the lamp with him, strode into the next room—leaving Amanda lying motionless in the darkness.

The blood was still pounding in her ears, and she was conscious of an overwhelmingly horrible sense of unfulfillment. But as the seconds ticked by and reality became clearer, she realized just what, in the heat of the moment, had almost happened. If it hadn't been for the ringing of the telephone . . .

Amanda groaned miserably and turned over, hiding her heated face with her hands. What kind of person was she? All her earlier years she had listened compassionately as friends confided their varied and sometimes traumatic experiences with sex. Privately she had always thought them sadly lacking in self-control. She had never had any problem along that line with Carl. Whenever his caresses became heated, a negative word from her stopped him. She herself had never been deeply stirred. But now . . . Oh, God! If he came back in and wanted to continue—

Tears of shame trickled down Amanda's cheeks, and a muffled sob racked her defenseless body. She wasn't sure what she would do. Being kissed and made love to by Boyd had evoked feelings she hadn't known she even possessed, and it seemed *her* control was more than sadly lacking—it was nonexistent.

"That was a friend of mine with the power company." The deep voice came from the doorway. "He said our lights will be back on in a few hours." Amanda could feel the force of the foreman's eyes on her back as she remained turned away and silent.

Several tense seconds passed before he continued, his tone tinged with bitterness. "I'm not going to apologize, Amanda. I didn't plan for that to happen, but I sure as hell enjoyed it—and so did you." When she made no reply, he sat the lantern on the chest and turned the wick down low.

"I'll leave this here with you," he stated roughly, his contempt for her childish attitude more than obvious. "Maybe it will keep the bogeyman away." Then he was gone and the room lost the spark of intensity his presence always seemed to bring.

For a long while afterward Amanda lay quietly on her bed, watching the faint golden glow of the lamp's rays on the ceiling, trying desperately to make her mind a complete blank.

## CHAPTER THREE

The next morning the happenings of the previous night could have been put down to some kind of nightmare if it were not for the mute evidence of the lantern as it still flickered its light against the brightness of the new day. Amanda stared at it dully, her remembered actions washing over her. An inarticulate cry rose to her lips as she almost jumped from the bed and hurried over to blow out the flame, as if doing so could ease her troubled spirit.

What was she to do? Could she possibly stay here now? And if she left, where would she go? The question ran repeatedly through her mind as she stood under the shower, letting the warm water soothe her overheated skin. A hotel? she wondered. But, no, there were no hotels near here—this was next door to the back of beyond. And another thought: if she did suddenly leave—go to another town, a large city—how could she possibly explain that action to Uncle John? He would be more than a little curious when he returned and found her gone. Not to mention the questions her father would ask. So, in a way, she was trapped! She would *have* to stay.

Amanda stepped from the shower stall and began to dry herself on one of the fluffy white towels lying stacked on a shelf. One thing was certain though. If she stayed, it would be vitally necessary for her not to let Boyd get near her again. And she would have to make it perfectly clear to him that last night was a mistake—one that was not going to be repeated.

And if he didn't listen? She shrugged lightly, holding the towel motionless in her hand—well, she could always threaten to tell her uncle he had tried to rape her, although she knew she would never follow through. For one thing, she hadn't a leg to stand on. She could have pulled away, or at least tried to fight him off with a little determination. But she had done neither. She had even encouraged him, enjoying his hot passionate kisses, his unforgettable touch.

The memory of the way his strong hands had moved urgently over her body made Amanda's breasts swell and the nipples grow taut. A warm curling feeling radiated through her body. God, when she remembered . . .

No, she hadn't tried to stop him—not at all—and that was the crux of the situation. For some reason that she couldn't understand, she was physically attracted to him. Maybe it was his devil-may-care attitude or the reckless streak that glittered in his unusually colored eyes. She didn't know, but she would definitely have to be on guard in the future. It couldn't happen again. Next time there might not be a saving interruption.

When she made her way to the kitchen, it was to find the foreman, sitting at the table, a cup of coffee nested in his hands, staring down into the murky depths as if the solution to an insurmountable problem might be found there. He glanced up when he sensed Amanda's presence, an aggrieved look in his pale eyes that pulled her up short. She hadn't expected to find him here, let alone for him to have that cold expression that bristled with hostility. His eyes were red-rimmed as if from lack of sleep, and she couldn't help wondering if he had been drinking after he left her last night. She wouldn't doubt it.

"Coffee?" he growled, and motioned to the percolator at his side.

"Yes, please." She slid gingerly into the chair across from him. She hadn't known exactly what to expect when they met again for the first time after what had happened last night, but she definitely had not expected this.

While stirring sugar into the hot liquid he poured she sent several questioning glances in his direction. But for the moment at least he seemed to have forgotten her presence.

When he did speak, the sudden breaking of the lengthy silence caused her hand to jerk, splashing a little of the coffee on the table.

"I'm moving my things back to the bunkhouse," he announced, his voice flat and emotionless.

"Oh?" Amanda swallowed, now looking anywhere but at him. She had known him in many moods in the short time since they had met, but this dark, uncommunicative one was entirely different. Maybe he, too, was regretting what had happened. Maybe he was afraid she would tell her uncle. But whatever the reason, it would solve her problem. With his disturbing presence removed from the house, she would be able to retain some kind of balance. And with Mrs. Gowen's return in the near future, things could possibly level off to some kind of normalcy. "Maybe that would be best," she replied slowly.

He pushed his cup away with an impatient hand and snorted, "Best! What an anemic way of putting things, Miss Reynolds." The look he gave her was enough to freeze her on the spot.

Amanda sat back in her chair, totally confused by the hostility being directed her way. He was acting as if everything that had happened was her fault!

A growing anger gave her the necessary courage to counter, "Yes, best. After last night, I *know* it would be. I don't want you in the house, Boyd. Even the bunkhouse is too close!"

A silence greeted her words. Then his drawling voice, smooth but with a wealth of meaning, said, "That's not the way you felt last night. In fact, I rather got the impression that you liked having me—close."

Amanda flushed to the roots of her blond curls, his mockery cutting into the shield she had tried to construct around her emotions. She lifted her chin in defiance.

"It was the storm. I've always been frightened of storms. It made me—" She paused to search for words.

"Uninhibited?" he supplied helpfully, the glacial air seeming to have changed like quicksilver into one of maddening humor.

"No, no—"

"Responsive?"

"*No!*" Amanda felt as if her entire body were on fire and not only from embarrassment. His softly spoken words were bringing back memories and, God help her, she was reacting. She shot a resentful glance at his long masculine form as he leaned back against his chair. A smile quirked up the corner of his mouth as his gaze roved over her heated face, seeming to uncover the thoughts and feelings she was experiencing.

"You took advantage of me!" she accused wildly.

"I didn't force you, lady."

The truth of his reply devastated her attack. What could she possibly answer? The only force exerted had been the power of their common need. If she had remained calm and cool, as she had always thought herself to be, none of it would have happened. Why did this man seem to get under her skin and show her glimpses of herself that she didn't even know existed? Damn and blast it! Why?

She was shifting uncomfortably in her chair when his taunting voice continued. "What's the matter? Are you sorry you found out you're a member of the human race?"

Amanda tipped her chin even farther up and glared at him.

"Don't look down that pretty little nose at me, honey." He laughed shortly. "I like you better when you're warm and soft and have lost your wings."

Amanda almost ground her teeth. If only she could hit him! But she was afraid that being the kind of man he was he would hit her right back. Instead, she settled for a blistering "Well, I don't like you—not at all! And—and I hope my uncle fires you!" Realizing she sounded all of ten years old didn't help Amanda's temper.

The calmness of the man's reply revealed his certainty of her answer. "When you tell him, are you going to tell him *everything*?"

Amanda's tawny eyes flashed but soon dropped in defeat. He knew she wouldn't. And since she had already decided that herself, she didn't understand her reason for threatening it. But the man confused and angered her, so the words had tumbled out without her willing them to.

"I didn't think so." He lighted a cigarette and exhaled the smoke slowly. "As I said before, I'm moving my things back to the bunkhouse—but it's not for your convenience. It's for mine." He flicked the extinguished match into an ashtray. "Since I don't think you're going to let me back into your bed again anytime soon and I fancy some sleep, I'm moving myself out of harm's way." The audacity of his remark had Amanda gasping. "I've been too damn short of sleep lately," he added darkly.

As if that were her fault too! Why the insufferable, arrogant—

A sharp rapping on the kitchen door broke into the tension vibrating in the air between them. When Amanda made no move to answer the summons, the foreman eased himself from his chair.

It was Jake Farling who waited outside. He nodded

shyly toward Amanda before starting to talk to the foreman in a hurried undertone. The foreman frowned, gave a curt nod, and told the man he would be right there. Then, after closing the door a bit, he reached for the Stetson that was conveniently resting on a hook behind it.

Amanda watched these quick economical movements and expected him to leave right away; but in this she was proved wrong. The man paused and glanced around. He didn't say anything, but the look he gave her centered on her parted lips and she could only gaze helplessly back, her mouth coming to tingling life as she remembered the touch of his. Hardly realizing what she was doing, she raised a wondering fingertip toward her chin.

At that revealing action a slow smile began to slant the corners of the foreman's attractive mouth and he gave a small satisfied nod before exiting, leaving Amanda to stare after him, irritation mingling liberally with excitement to make her golden eyes as bright as gemstones.

That day proved to be another restless one for Amanda. She tried to sketch, but all she came up with after many attempts was an assortment of half-finished drawings of cattle and fences, an occasional clump of prickly pear, and some of the outbuildings of the ranch. The image of a certain cowboy seemed to be indelibly engraved on her mind's eye, and she could settle on nothing else. Finally she gave up and began to play with quickly drawn lines, and to her surprise and amazement the result was the best study of a person she had ever done. Somehow she had captured the essence of the man, his confident, virile, much-too-disturbing masculine self: the steady, sometimes mocking eyes; the sensual curve of his hard, firm lips. Her first inclination was to tear it to shreds. It was too darn much like him! Then she looked at it again and inexplicably buried it deep in the back pages of her sketch-pad.

She had just come inside from sitting on the front porch when the telephone began to ring. She hesitated, feeling a little funny about answering someone else's phone, then castigated herself for her silliness. Who else was there to answer it? She picked it up and said "Hello?"

"Hello?" the voice repeated. It was that of an older woman.

"Yes?" Amanda tried again.

"Who is this? Is that Miss Reynolds?"

Amanda smiled faintly. At least the person on the other end knew who *she* was. "Yes, this is Amanda Reynolds. Who is this, please?"

"What?" The gravelly voice rose impatiently. "I can't hear you. Speak up, girl."

Amanda did as she was directed, realizing that the woman must have a hearing problem. "I said, 'Yes, this is Amanda Reynolds.' Who is this?"

"You don't have to yell. My hearing aid is working now," came the testy reply.

Amanda had to cover her mouth with her hand in an attempt to stifle a giggle. "I'm sorry," she said.

The woman seemed to be mollified. "This is Hazel Gowen, John Reynolds's housekeeper. I'm calling from Craigmont Hospital. They brought me to this confounded place even though I told them that I wasn't hurt much. Now they seem determined to keep me. Roary too. Now, young lady, how are things going at the ranch? Has Josh Taylor been over to see you yet? He promised he would keep an eye on you." The woman didn't wait for a reply, but went on. "I tell you, we have had more problems this year! First one of the coldest winters on record then one of the driest springs and summers—and now this accident. Roary's in a worse temper than I am. Keeps thinking what

61

a load Josh is carrying, what with looking after both ranches . . ." Finally she paused for breath. But just as Amanda thought it safe to make a reply, the woman cut in demandingly, "Are you still there?"

"Yes, ma'am. I—"

"Good. For a minute I thought we'd been disconnected. Now, have you been able to get yourself comfortable?"

"Er—yes," Amanda answered quickly. "Yes, I have." The woman sounded like a veritable dynamo. If she ran the ranch house the way she talked, it was no wonder her Uncle John was afraid the place would fall apart if she decided to leave.

The woman grunted approval and asked, "Have you seen Josh Taylor?"

Amanda frowned. She had no idea who the different people were to whom the housekeeper kept referring. "No, no, I've met no one but the foreman and one of the men— Jake someone."

"What?" the gruff voice was raised again. "Just a minute."

Amanda waited while a muffled thumping noise came through the earpiece.

"Dratted hearing aid," the woman grumbled. "Thing's never worked right. Now, look, young lady. Sounds are a little garbled, so I'll do all the talking."

Amanda wisely kept quiet and refrained from observing humorously that that had been the case all along.

"Now, I plan to be home Saturday no matter what that doctor says. In the meantime, if you need anything, you'll find Josh's number written on the list by the hall phone. I can't understand him not coming by. Oh, and if you see him, be sure to tell him Roary says thanks again for seeing to that bull. Roary was mighty worried on the way to my sister's. Says that's why he didn't see that car pull out on us. Well, I'll let you go for now. The nurse is wheeling in

62

some of that stuff they call food here. Mind you, tell Josh what Roary said. . . ." The voice trailed off as Amanda heard another voice in the background giving instructions and the housekeeper's demanding request for a repetition. Then the disconnecting click left Amanda bemusedly looking down at the now-dead instrument. Meeting Hazel Gowen was definitely going to be an experience! But who was the Roary she kept talking about? Another one of the hired hands? And who was Josh Taylor?

She shrugged her slim shoulders and shook her head. Lord, if there was one thing she didn't need, it was more men on the scene. The foreman was enough—more than enough—and Saturday seemed a long time away!

It must have been her afternoon for calls, because not long after talking to Hazel the telephone rang again. Amanda answered it with more confidence this time and found herself talking to her uncle. His reason for calling was almost identical to his housekeeper's, asking if she was settling in all right and telling her that he would see her sometime next week. At the end of the call he also mentioned Josh Taylor, telling her to be especially nice to him—that he was a good friend. Then he said good-bye and Amanda was left to wonder once again about the paragon of virtue named Josh.

The foreman came back to the house just as the sun was setting in the western sky. He looked tired and dirty and more than a little disgusted. But when he smelled the delicious aroma of the stew Amanda was preparing, his white teeth flashed in a crooked smile and he said, "No hot sauce, I hope."

It was as if he were willing her to a temporary truce by calling back to mind the camaraderie they had shared for a short time the previous evening, before things had started to get out of hand.

Amanda smiled slightly in response, but still retained a measure of wariness. "Only a little."

"Then I guess I'll have to trust you, because I'm starving. I am invited . . . ?" He left the question hanging.

Amanda nodded stiffly. She had made more than enough and couldn't honestly tell herself that she had not planned for this very eventuality. She might dislike the man, but she could still see the need for providing him with a meal. After all, he was her uncle's foreman.

He tapped the worn Stetson on the side of his lean thigh before hanging it on the waiting hook. "Have I got enough time to get my things?"

Amanda kept her back to him. For the sake of this temporary truce it was better if she did. "Yes. It will be about another ten minutes." She didn't look around as he moved out of the room.

He returned when the meal was ready. As Amanda poured the iced tea, she noted that somewhere in those ten minutes he had found time to shower and change. His dun-colored jeans hugged his long legs tightly and the dark blue shirt he was wearing was casually tailored to his wide shoulders, emphasizing the lightness of his pale eyes. And he had shaved, exuding a faint woodsy aroma.

As the meal progressed she felt his eyes travel over her occasionally, but she steadfastly refused to meet them. He was something of a sleeping tiger: one wrong move and an unwary lamb would be devoured. She told herself repeatedly that she had no desire to be that lamb—but she couldn't help the surging awareness his closeness brought.

The stew was tasteless to her, but he seemed to be enjoying it. He was just finishing his second helping when Amanda brought up the subject of her call from the housekeeper, more to break the mounting tension she was feeling than anything else.

"Hazel called," he repeated, his eyes narrowed on her small face.

"Yes. She says she'll be back here Saturday."

He merely grunted.

"Uncle John called too."

A dark eyebrow rose.

"He said that he'll be back late next week."

A sarcastic smile broke across the man's hard face as he drawled mockingly, "Then you'll be all safe and sound. Will you like that, Amanda?"

Amanda's face flushed as she tried to ignore his inference. "Boyd"—she was desperate to get them on some other subject. "Who's Josh Taylor?"

The man's body seemed to stiffen slightly, and his smile slowly disappeared. "Why do you want to know?" he asked.

"Well, Mrs. Gowen said he was supposed to come by." Her curiosity made her go on. "Has he?"

"Yes." The reply was abrupt.

"Did he want to see me?"

"No. He just came by to see about the ranch."

"Who is he, then? A neighbor?"

He nodded his head impatiently, as if talking about Josh Taylor was not his favorite pastime.

"Was it today?" Amanda asked after a brief pause.

"Yesterday."

"Oh." She felt very out of her depth in the face of his terse replies. "Well, if you see him again, I'm supposed to give him a message."

The foreman watched her so steadily that Amanda found herself compelled to continue. "Mrs. Gowen said a Roary someone-or-other wants to thank him for helping with a bull. Boyd, who's Roary?" Nervousness made her laugh self-consciously. "I don't seem to know anyone, do I?"

The foreman didn't laugh with her. Instead an unreadable gleam came into his eyes as he stated quietly, "You know me."

A quiver of emotion ran through Amanda as her startled gaze flew to his lean, tanned face and met the pale light of his eyes. Immediately she was caught by the strong force of his attraction.

"But then I guess I don't count for much," he went on. "I'm just a poor, working cowboy."

Sometimes talking with him was like trying to find your way out of a maze! "What?" she asked. "I don't understand."

"Josh Taylor. He's one of the wealthiest ranchers in this part of Texas. Women come from miles around just to throw themselves at him. And parents push their willing daughters."

Amanda was taken momentarily aback at the bitterness she had inadvertently loosened. Was he jealous of Josh Taylor? He sounded as if he hated him! Or was it just the fact that the man was nearby competition and had the winning combination of money and power?

She tried to think of something to say. He seemed to be waiting. In the end she knew what she came up with sounded trite and ineffectual, but it was the best she could do: "Money isn't everything, Boyd. It's what's inside a person that counts."

Silver eyes glittered into her own as he grated caustically. "Obviously I'm talking to an angel again. Got your wings back on, Amanda? I don't suppose *you* would ever be interested in marrying a man just for his money."

"No, I don't think so," she answered, still reeling from the harshness of his attack.

The foreman watched her keenly, leaning his crossed arms on the table. "Are you so very different then? Are

66

you saying that if a poor man like me asked you to marry him, you would? No questions asked?"

Amanda hesitated, a strong sense of unreality taking root in her mind. "Yes, I—I think so. If I—"

She was allowed to go no further. "Prove it," he shot back.

"What?"

"I said, prove it."

Amanda's heart skidded to a full stop, then started up again with pounding speed. She swallowed and whispered tightly, "I don't think I understand."

"Tell me you'll marry me—that my being poor doesn't matter to you."

A sinking feeling settled in the pit of Amanda's stomach. What kind of a mess had she got herself into this time?

"Boyd! You're not being fair. I—I couldn't marry you. I've just met you!"

"Does time make that much difference?"

She tried, but still could not read the expression in his eyes. "Yes—no. I don't know!" She almost wailed. He was confusing her again, leaning toward her with his silver-gray eyes fixed firmly on her face. She dragged her eyes away with an effort and concentrated on the darkness outside the window. She was trembling as his soft, persuasive voice continued.

"Sometimes it happens like that, Amanda. Two people meet and immediately they know they belong together."

Wide, frightened eyes turned back to him. "Are you trying to tell me that you—that I—"

"Stranger things have happened." He sat back in his seat. "And we're not exactly what could be called incompatible in bed."

A mounting panic made her ask, "Is that all you can

think about?" Her cheeks were hot, and her fingers began plucking nervously at a speck on the tablecloth.

His answer came with a maddening half smile. "On occasion I think about other things."

"You're crazy."

"Not any more than you are."

"But—"

"You still haven't answered my question." He shrugged his shoulders negligently. "It can be hypothetical, if you like."

"Hypothetical?"

"For me, substitute any man in my position."

Amanda expelled her breath in one long hiss. He was playing with her! All along, it had just been a game to him. A surge of white-hot anger shook her to the center of her being. Never had she felt such intense negative emotion. Two vivid spots of color were high on her cheeks, and her golden eyes flashed with molten fire. Once again he had used her for bait.

"All right, all right! I'll answer you. No! No, I would never marry you—or anyone like you. You're everything I despise in a man." She paused for breath, uncaring of the stillness that had come over him. "I would have to be insane to want to marry someone like you." She waved an expressive hand in the air. "Never knowing when you'd come home drunk—or be carried home. Never knowing what woman you picked up for the night. No—just bring on your wealthy rancher. If I got lucky and he wanted to marry me, I'd accept in a second."

The foreman was instantly on his feet, ignoring the crash his chair made as it fell to the floor. Two large hands whipped out to grasp Amanda by the shoulders, digging into the soft flesh unmercifully.

"You're just like every other woman, aren't you? You mouth such sweet little platitudes—'It's what's inside a

68

person that counts.' " He uttered an ugly expletive. "Money—that's what talks to women like you. But answer this: Can all the money in the world keep you warm at night, can it make you feel as if you're going to explode with desire if it doesn't hurry up and take possession of you? I know I made you feel that way last night. And I know I can make you feel it again!"

Amanda's startled gasp was cut off as his mouth came down with brutal intent, meant to silence any protest. It crushed savagely against her own, forcing her head back —grinding the tender skin of her lips against her teeth— while the steellike muscles of his arms strained her close against the rock-hard outline of his form.

At first Amanda was incapable of any reaction other than shock, the suddenness of his assault taking her by storm. But as seconds spun by, her mental paralysis lifted and she began to struggle. Only as she did, his tactics changed. He eased back, savage demand conceding to expert sensual persuasion—the warm movements of his lips coaxing, prompting, willing her to arousal, the strong hands on her back caressing rather than biting.

And in spite of herself Amanda started to respond. She felt as if she had been thrust into the giant ocean of desire and were drowning in dangerous excitement. Her body ceased all sign of protest to melt against his as she surrendered to dizzying waves of enjoyment, the slow-burning fire only he was capable of igniting conflagrating into open flame.

A delicious quiver rippled up her spine when, as her mouth parted to receive the moist intimacy of his tongue, a low husky groan escaped deep from his throat.

She raised her arms that had been imprisoned against his chest and twined them around his neck, her fingers playing in the thickness of his hair above his collar. At the same time, his work-calloused hands slid down the length of her body to the gentle swell of her hips to pull her close—making her overwhelmingly aware of his need.

Amanda began to tremble, her senses stirred to fever pitch. She wanted him just as badly as he wanted her.

Then as suddenly as the kiss began, it ended, and she was pushed violently away.

"I'll remember what you said, Amanda," the foreman grated, his breathing ragged, his silver eyes still shimmering from the height of his stimulation. "Maybe next time you'll be more willing to listen. But, then again, maybe I won't feel like talking."

After giving her one last all-encompassing look, he turned and walked from the house.

Amanda remained where she was, stunned by the harshness of his words and stricken by his abrupt withdrawal. All at once she began to tremble more severely and a trickle of tears started to roll down over her cheeks.

How could she have reacted to him the way she had—twice! And with such unbridled unrestraint? She didn't love him! She didn't even like him! What she felt could only be described as one thing—lust! And that was against everything she had ever believed.

Amanda sniffed loudly and impotently tried to stem the flow of tears.

## CHAPTER FOUR

Wednesday and Thursday of that week passed with agonizing slowness for Amanda. The foreman was noticeable only by his absence, and the only other human contact she had was an occasional glimpse of Jake Farling as he made his way about the outer yard. At one time she had wondered where the man lived—if he, too, lived in the bunkhouse—but later she found out that he rented a small place from her uncle that was located some distance away from the ranch house. He had a wife and a son and seemed totally content with his life. Something that Amanda at the moment was not. All her attempts at concentrating on sketching came to the same end—mounds of balled-up paper on the ground around her in a wholly unsatisfying mess.

By Friday morning she had had enough. After slipping into a pair of white slacks and donning a bright blue print blouse that had been a present from her father on her birthday, she drove into Craigmont, which as far as she could tell from the map was about twenty miles away.

It was not a very large town; in fact, it didn't merit more than a tiny dot on the Texas map, but Amanda enjoyed her morning there because in many ways its small-town atmosphere reminded her of Kemperville. She looked into most of the stores lining the main street and found that the people were friendly. But when they discovered that she was John Reynolds's niece, they became even more welcoming. Repeatedly she heard the same commiserating remarks about Hazel Gowen and the man named Roary. Amanda would nod and repeat the same sentences again and again, that yes, it was too bad the accident had happened and yes, she was getting along fine on her own. When she once mentioned to a storekeeper that the foreman was there for company, the man she was talking to looked at her strangely and started to question her further, but the arrival of a customer asking for help halted him, and the question was forgotten.

Amanda played with the idea of going to the hospital to visit Hazel and the mysterious Roary, but in the end she decided not to. The woman was coming back to the ranch tomorrow—there would be time enough then to meet her.

She had lunch in a small café that was run by a local family and delighted at the stories the oldest member, a man of ninety or so years, told her of the history of the town and its inhabitants, notably her uncle and his past transgressions when, as a young man, he was fresh from Dallas—and a little wild in the bargain.

She was laughing at one of the more outrageous episodes when the café door opened, and who but the foreman should walk in. He looked almost as surprised as Amanda, and for a moment she thought he was going to walk out. But then, as if coming to a decision, he moved directly across the room to her side.

"Amanda," he said in greeting, his pale eyes running over her features in a lightning glance that took in the remnants of her laughter.

Amanda twitched uneasily in her chair, and murmured a noncommittal greeting. The old man rose and, straightening to his full bowed height, reached with one long thin arm to shake hands.

72

"Haven't seen you around here in a long time, son," The reedy voice was alive with pleasure.

"How're you making it, Grandpa?" The foreman smiled back warmly.

Grandpa Wilson was called that by all the townspeople. It was as if, by being the oldest resident, he had been adopted by everyone.

"Right fine, son, right fine." Bleary blue eyes, lighted with gleeful amusement, turned on Amanda. "I might have known you'd already know this pretty little thing. Come on," he said, waving his hand to an empty chair, "have a seat. Margaret!" he called. "Get us some coffee." A young girl Amanda had earlier been introduced to as his granddaughter, promptly disappeared behind a swinging door.

The foreman's worn hat was resting on the table as he leaned back in his chair. When the girl approached, he removed it, giving it a place on his lap. Margaret smiled at him shyly as she filled each cup and blushed a fiery red when he smiled his thanks. That devastating charm worked even on fourteen-year-olds, Amanda thought sourly as she took a hasty sip of her coffee, then had to cough because it burned her mouth.

A dark eyebrow rose tauntingly, almost disappearing under the thatch of dark, curling hair that had fallen over his forehead. It was all Amanda could do not to kick him under the table. She had come here to get away from him—and now here he was, continuing to mock her and to set her pulse leaping!

With as much haughty disdain as she could muster, Amanda returned his look. But that only caused his smile to broaden further until the two intriguing creases in both sides of his cheeks became prominent.

Infuriated, Amanda turned to the old man. "Grandpa, you were telling me about my uncle . . ." she prompted.

The old man grinned, showing a white expanse of false teeth. "Oh, I was done, child. I think I've told you just about everything." His lively eyes swung to the foreman and soon began to twinkle. "But this one here"—a gnarled hand motioned to their companion—"lordy, I could go on all day about him! Led his mama a terrible life when he was a boy."

The foreman's steady eyes smiled across at the old man. "We wouldn't want to bore the lady, Grandpa," he drawled.

The old man laughed delightedly. "I get it. I'll keep quiet for now. But it's only because it's getting time for my afternoon siesta." He patted Amanda on the hand. "Next time I'll tell you all about Josh here. Sometime when he's not around."

Slowly, with protesting muscles and joints, the old man got to his feet. "Been nice meeting you, John's niece. Come again and see us before you leave. Bye, Josh." And with that he moved away.

Amanda was as still as if she had been turned into an ice sculpture. She watched with stolid concentration as the old man slowly crossed the room. Then wide golden eyes that were slightly dazed turned to the man sitting across from her. He was in the process of lighting a cigarette, his long fingers cupping the match to the tip. When he was done, he leaned back in his chair and lazily threw an estimating glance across the distance between them.

Amanda's face was pale, and she had to clear her throat before she could speak. She felt as if someone had delivered a blow to her solar plexus and she was still reeling, trying to regain her breath.

"What did he call you?" she asked faintly, disbelievingly.

The man's eyes narrowed. "What do you think he called me?"

Amanda was silent for a moment then said, "He called you Josh!"

"Then I guess that's who I am." The words were spoken so softly that Amanda had to strain to hear them, but hear them she did, and a swift anger began to burn. Her fists clenched and unclenched and she took a deep breath before saying loudly, forgetting the other people in the room. "Why of all the—"

The words ended in a surprised gurgle as a large hand shot out to grip her wrist tightly.

"Not in here!" he stated fiercely.

Amanda was shocked into silence, then noticed that heads had turned in their direction.

Angrily she hissed back, "Then you'd better find somewhere quick, because I don't plan to wait very long."

The threat implicit in her words held no terror for him. It was as if he had only stopped her earlier to save her embarrassment. Slowly and with maddening calm he crushed out the cigarette he had just lighted and motioned for the young girl to bring the bill.

"I'll pay for mine!" Amanda insisted, but was ignored.

Walking stiffly behind him, Amanda glowered at his broad back. Oh, how she despised him! All along he had been playing with her! *He* was Josh Taylor! The rich, much-lauded Josh Taylor. How he must have laughed when she all but accused him of being a lush!

Once outside the door Amanda took a breath to begin but was once again halted by a terse "Not yet."

With that he ushered her toward a late-model tan and brown station wagon that was sitting at the curb; without much gentleness he pushed her inside. He then came around to the driver's side, and before she quite knew what was happening, he had started the engine and they were leaving the small town behind.

"What are you doing now? Kidnapping me?" she demanded, her golden eyes sparkling with fury.

He spared her a withering glance before turning his attention back to the road. Amanda threw herself angrily back against the seat and crossed her arms over her heaving breast.

They drove in silence for several miles before he turned the car off the road and parked it to one side of a group of stubby trees. A small stream gurgled down a nearby rocky incline and lost itself under the narrow bridge on the roadway only to reappear again on the other side.

"Well?" she demanded. "May I talk now?" Her request was rich with sarcasm.

"If you think you have to," the man replied quietly, as he leaned back in his seat and turned intent gray eyes on her small furious face.

Amanda was amazed at the range of emotions this man could arouse in her.

"Oh, I think I do. Would you mind telling me just who the holy hell you are?"

"Don't swear," he instructed.

"I'll swear if I *damn* well want to!"

"You're acting like a child." His rational calmness made Amanda want to hit something good and hard—preferably the man sitting next to her. When he saw that she was almost beside herself, he relented somewhat and smiled slightly. "Would it help if I use the old cliché and tell you you're beautiful when you're angry?"

"Why did you tell me you were Boyd?" she demanded.

"If you'll think back a little, you'll find I never did. You were the one who insisted I was Boyd—along with a few other things."

Amanda let that barbed comment pass. "But you let me believe—"

"Only because you wanted to so badly."

76

"Why you—" At last Amanda's control evaporated, and her hand snaked out, catching his lean hard cheek in a resounding slap.

For a moment the experience was all she had thought it would be. She was filled with a heady sense of exhilaration; but when she saw the effect her action had on the man, her hand suddenly dropped to her lap, there to be squeezed tightly by the other.

Where at one time he had been willing to talk to her as if addressing an enraged eight-year-old—and not without a sprinkling of humor—he now had stiffened and the anger that blazed from his eyes as they held her own caused her breath to catch in her throat.

"Why you spoiled little bitch," he rasped out harshly. "All right, if that's the way you want it—" He took her by the shoulders and pulled her across the seat until she was hard against his body. "You asked for this," he murmured. The merciless kiss that followed was filled only with anger, and this time there was no softening into persuasion. A hand was transferred to the back of her head and threaded into her curls, forcing her even closer. Amanda felt the skin of her lips give and tasted the salt of her blood. Tears of pain began to escape from her closed eyes.

Almost immediately she was flung away to the accompaniment of an angry oath. His breathing was labored as he rested his forehead on arms curved around the steering wheel—as if that object were the only stable thing in a world gone suddenly mad.

"Sometimes I think I could almost kill you," he breathed harshly. As the softly spoken words came to Amanda's ears she cringed slightly. She believed him!

He raised his head, his cold gray eyes searching her face, running over the golden curls, and settling on her swollen

77

mouth. Some deep emotion surfaced momentarily in their depths but was quickly hidden.

"I never set out to deceive you, Amanda," he stated quietly, his voice sounding inordinately weary.

"Take me back to my car, please," Amanda whispered unsteadily, her head bowed, rejecting him, rejecting his words.

The man sighed deeply. "Not until we've had a chance to talk."

"I don't want to talk!" A flare of anger kindled, then died. "I—I just want to go home."

Tears sparkled in her gold-flecked eyes as she looked at him. Josh Taylor saw them and with another smothered curse started the car's engine.

The trip back to town was accomplished with great speed.

When he spotted her car parked in one of the slots in front of the drugstore, he braked to a stop. "Do you think you can drive?" he asked, his words toneless, impersonal —as if his anger were still barely under control and he didn't trust himself to show any form of emotion.

"Yes," she said huskily, and began to open the door.

But when she made a move to step out, his voice stopped her. "I'm following you home, Amanda."

Amanda only nodded dully, her emotions having played themselves out, leaving her exhausted.

During the long drive back to her uncle's ranch Amanda was conscious of the large station wagon that followed closely behind. A mistiness came to her eyes several times, but she determinedly blinked it away. Home! How she wished she were going home. There were fewer problems there than here! Less danger. But at the moment she didn't want to think, to feel. She wanted to be just like Scarlett O'Hara in *Gone with the Wind*—she wanted to think about it tomorrow.

78

But her desire was not to be. For that night, as she lay awake in bed, she slowly regained some semblance of feeling. And instead of experiencing the predominant emotion of anger, she found that she was thoroughly confused. So much had happened since coming to the ranch. She had run away from Carl and her love of him only to find herself under the direct influence of a man she had thought to be the foreman—a drunk, a no-good, a man who had been in trouble with the police and who thought women were there for the taking. And now she found that she had been mistaken. That somehow, through her own false assumptions, she had drawn a hasty conclusion. Was that why everyone she had talked to about the foreman had acted so strangely? Just who was the foreman?

But none of that mattered as much as her totally inexplicable response to the man. All he had to do was look at her and she became one gigantic mass of quivering Jell-O. Her cool, usually controlled emotions took a flying leap out the nearest window, and she reacted like some sort of sex-starved female. Was it something basic to her character that was touched by his undoubtedly masculine virility? When he was talking about the phantom Josh Taylor, he himself had said Josh had his choice of women.

So why had he gone along with the pretense of being Boyd? Her entire body burned with embarrassment as she remembered her angry reply to his fake proposal. "Bring on your wealthy rancher," she had challenged. Well, he was there, only she hadn't known it! Was that the reason for his mysterious reply? That next time she might be willing to listen, but he might not feel like talking. Had he known then that with Hazel and later her uncle coming back, his masquerade would soon be over? Had it all been some kind of test to see if she would agree to marry him when she thought him poor? But if that was so, what purpose had it served? He certainly didn't love her—not any more than she loved him!

With that thought Amanda turned over onto her side and buried her head in her pillow. Her mouth was still tender from his savage kiss and emotionally she felt just as bruised. She was confused and she was tired and what she wanted more than anything else in the entire world right then was the blessed oblivion of sleep.

## CHAPTER FIVE

Hazel Gowen was everything Amanda had thought she would be: gruff, abrupt, intolerant of fools, hard of hearing in one ear with an aid—which didn't always function—occasionally positioned in the other, and wonderfully loyal to John Reynolds. One of the first things the housekeeper did when she entered the house that Saturday morning was to limp to the kitchen with the help of a cane, pull an apron from a drawer, and tie it around her narrow waist as if it were a badge of office.

She was a small woman with gray-streaked black hair and a trim figure that did nothing to help an onlooker guess her age. Her face had some lines—but not many—and as her sharp brown eyes ran over Amanda she nodded with approval.

"Thanks for seeing to the house while I was away," she stated.

Amanda smiled, "It wasn't hard. It was in such good order when I came."

"All the same, thank you. Now, what would you like for dinner tonight?"

Amanda started to protest, "Oh, but you don't have to do that. I mean, it's your first day back, and you probably should rest."

The brown eyes flashed and Amanda subsided. "Young

woman, I'm a person who *needs* to work. Now, what would you like? How about a nice roast?"

Amanda quickly gave her approval and left the room. She knew her offer of help would be rejected. The captain was back at the ship's helm, and it was time for the first officer to step down—gracefully.

Later that night, over a delicious dinner of roast beef with potatoes and carrots and a tossed green salad, Hazel told an interested Amanda about the accident that had occurred to herself and the real foreman, Roary Boyd.

It seemed that the foreman, described as a lean man in his late fifties who had a rapidly receding hairline of sandy blond hair, had been driving Hazel into Craigmont for her weekly visit to her sister when a car had unexpectedly come out of a side road, failed to yield to a stop sign, and plowed into the side of their pickup. Promptly their truck had overturned—something, Hazel said, she never wanted to experience again—and in the process had shaken both occupants thoroughly. The result had been a shattered leg for Roary and an assortment of cuts and bruises along with a badly wrenched knee for herself.

Moreover, Hazel and Roary had never been in a hospital a day in their lives and apparently did not take their enforced stay with good grace.

"They make Roary stay in bed—he can't do much of anything except watch TV," Hazel commiserated sadly. "He doesn't like to read." An amused smile began to play about her lips. "The other day the nurse told me that his TV went out in the middle of one of his soap operas. She said the air was pretty blue until someone came in with another set. It was the only way they could shut him up." She laughed heartily. "Men! Many's the time Roary's laughed at me for wanting to see my favorite doctor show. Now he doesn't have any room to talk."

82

Amanda smiled at the triumph in Hazel's tone. Roary, it seemed, would never live down the tale.

Hazel soon sobered. "I'll have to go back in to see him now and again until his leg is well enough for him to come back home. It isn't any fun being cooped up in that place."

Amanda felt a sense of shame run through her at Hazel's words. Yesterday in Craigmont she had thought about going to the hospital and visiting the housekeeper but had shied away from it. Now she was saddened that she had not. The woman wasn't nearly as fierce as she had sounded on the telephone. "I'm sorry I didn't come to see you, Hazel," she began hesitantly, "I—"

She didn't get any further. A hand rose imperiously to quiet her. "I can't stand visitors. All they do is fidget and make me nervous. After the first day, I told the doctor I didn't want to see anyone, and I didn't."

The information made Amanda feel a little better.

When they were almost finished with the meal, Hazel asked, "Did you ever see Josh Taylor?"

Amanda's fork clattered to the table before falling onto the floor. As she bent to retrieve it she tried to calm her unsteady nerves. Color filled her cheeks, and Hazel looked at her curiously.

"Uh, yes," she murmured.

The housekeeper pursed her lips. "Did you tell him what I told you to?"

Amanda frowned slightly, feeling flustered. "What?"

"About the bull."

"Oh. Oh, no—yes. I mean—"

Hazel clucked her tongue. "Just like your uncle. He can't remember what day it is sometimes. Are you an artist too? No, never mind. I expect you are. No matter. But if you don't mind, I'd like you to drive me over to the Taylor place tomorrow."

The blood drained from Amanda's face. "Over—over to the Taylors'?" she repeated stupidly.

"What's the matter with you, girl? Do you need one of these?" Hazel tapped her right ear.

In her agitation Amanda had a saving idea. "He—Josh —has been over here almost every day since I came. Couldn't you see him when he comes again? I mean—"

"No, I could not! That man's gone out of his way to help us. It's the least I can do to thank him properly. And anyway, it's not only Josh I want to see. It's his mother. Wonderful woman, Megan Taylor. She's not been feeling too strong lately, and I want to see how she's doing."

At that Amanda hung her head in defeat. The trip was inevitable. Just as were her further dealings with the man. There seemed to be very little she could do about it.

Early the next afternoon, after spending the morning attending a local church service with Hazel, Amanda followed the housekeeper's halting steps as she walked up a pathway leading to a house that was twice the size of her uncle's but built of the same stone. It appeared to have been constructed at about the same period, and Amanda wondered how many generations of Taylors had lived there. Somehow she didn't think they were newcomers to the hard rugged land, as her uncle had been a number of years ago. Their roots probably went deep.

After knocking once on the massive front door, Hazel pushed it open a crack and called inside. "Megan?"

An answering call from within had Hazel completing the opening of the door and walking in. "It's me—Hazel."

"Hazel! Oh, come in, come in." The soft musical voice was warm and happy.

Hesitantly Amanda followed the housekeeper into the house and with wide eyes saw the comfort the large living room offered. The furnishings were functional, the autumn colors pleasing to the eye. A bookcase lining one side of the wall was filled with books and prized possessions, and a painting that could only have been done by her uncle was hanging on the opposite wall.

So this was where Josh Taylor lived, Amanda thought tautly as she took in the cane rocking chair and the thick glass top of an occasional table positioned in front of a sectional couch. It was not exactly what she had expected, and yet again it was. Josh Taylor didn't give the appearance of being rich and neither did his home. It had a kind of understated elegance that was occasionally deceptive. Then her eyes caught sight of a pack of cigarettes along with a set of keys lying on a small table beside the outer door, and she knew they could belong to only one person. At any moment she expected him to come striding in, asking furiously why she was there. They had not parted on the best of terms the last time they met, and only a crazy person would come defenseless to the enemy's stronghold.

She started guiltily when Hazel touched her arm and said, "This way."

They went down a long hall and into a spacious bedroom that was a reflection of the warm pretty woman who was lying propped against two pillows in the center of an oversize bed. A light pink coverlet was spread over her lower limbs and a cloud of white hair created a nimbus around her thin, delicate face. Pale blue-gray eyes looked from Hazel to Amanda. "You didn't tell me you were bringing company, Hazel," she protested good-naturedly.

"This is Amanda Reynolds, Megan. John's niece."

A frail hand reached out to take Amanda's, and she was conscious of the almost too-cool touch. "Amanda, welcome. Come, sit down, both of you . . . please."

Amanda smiled tremulously. Megan Taylor looked almost too fragile to be Josh Taylor's mother—too gentle. Yet, the pale eyes, as they watched her move to take her place in the straight-backed chair, went over her with the same intentness as her son's. Amanda felt an almost physical relief when they turned toward the housekeeper.

"Hazel, it's so good to see you! You must tell me everything that's happened to you. Josh told me a little, but he tries to keep me from getting upset, so he leaves out important details. How are you, dear? Is your knee very painful? And how is Roary?"

Hazel answered the barrage of questions with good humor, skimming over the horror of the accident and dwelling instead on Roary's and her own experiences in the hospital. It was as if she were also trying to protect the woman from the harsher facts of the misadventure.

Megan Taylor listened then sympathized. "I know how that can be." She shook her head. "I've spent too many days in a hospital myself. Oh, the nurses and doctors are wonderful, but it's just not home—and nothing they do can make it be. Did you feel that way?"

Hazel agreed. "Most definitely. I was never so glad to be away from a place in all my life."

The pale eyes turned back to Amanda; but instead of the cool estimating look she was expecting, they were alight with warm humor.

"Don't let two old women bore you, Amanda. We can compare horror stories some other time. Now, tell me about you. Are you visiting your uncle for the summer or do you plan to stay longer? I think it would be good for him if you did stay awhile."

Amanda responded to the friendly interest and told a heavily censored version of leaving her job at the bank with the idea of attempting a career in art.

Megan's face lighted up. "Why, that's wonderful. Another Reynolds artist! Your uncle is our pride and joy

86

around here, you know. A long time ago I had a crush on him—before I married Josh's father—but John was already head-over-heels in love with someone else and couldn't see me at all, although he did lose her -" She sighed at her memories. "But it all worked out in the end. Charles made me forget all about John—in that sense at least."

Privately Amanda couldn't help but think that if the father was anything like his son, she could see how it had happened. Even in his sixties her Uncle John was still a handsome man, and she knew from family pictures that he had been even more so when younger. But if Josh Taylor took after his father—a foregone conclusion, since he certainly didn't look a thing like his mother—then Charles Taylor could have won any girl he chose with very little effort. Look what Josh had done to her!

Horrified at the conclusion her mind had drawn, Amanda pulled herself up short. Her heart began to beat in double time, and it seemed as if she were at the edge of some kind of precipice. But when Megan's voice continued, asking as if from a distance if they would like some refreshments, she felt the sudden dizziness recede.

"Er . . . yes. That would be nice," she agreed in a slightly dazed manner.

The visit was almost safely at an end, and Amanda had at last relaxed sufficiently to stop jumping at each strange noise, knowing that the housekeeper-companion-nurse she had met earlier was busy working about the house, when Megan's delighted voice caused her to close her eyes in momentary dismay.

"Oh, Josh!" Megan cried, holding out her hand. "Come look who's visiting."

The tall figure of the man paused for a fraction of a second before moving fully into the room. His large hand enfolded his mother's frail one then released it. "Morning, Hazel, good to see you back. Amanda."

A quick glance had Amanda sliding her eyes away. If anything, he was even handsomer than she remembered. His hair was brushed into obedience, and he was dressed in a dark suit with a white shirt that emphasized his tanned skin; it was all she could do not to stare.

"I didn't know you knew Amanda, Josh," his mother said. "Oh, but I guess you do since she's been staying at John's."

The silver eyes flickered over Amanda's denim skirt and white embroidered blouse. "We've met," he answered noncommittally.

"Josh." Hazel drew his attention. "Roary wanted me to thank you again for all you did for that bull. Jim Bishop told him how you were up all night with it and how sorry he was that he was away when he was needed. But Roary and he agreed that if anyone could have saved the animal, it was you. You've always had a way with them." In an aside Hazel explained to Amanda, "Jim Bishop is our vet."

"I did what I could." Josh seemed ill at ease with the sincerity of the compliment.

"But if you hadn't stayed with the animal, it might have died. You couldn't have gotten a wink of sleep that night."

Josh shrugged, but his mother spoke up. "He didn't. Came back here the next afternoon looking like some kind of surly outlaw. And then he wouldn't stay. Just gave some instructions to Frank and some of the men and left again. Were you there, Amanda, when all of this was happening?"

Amanda swallowed hastily, darting another glance at Josh. Upon encountering his stony countenance, she turned back to his mother's questioning face. Had that been the morning of her arrival? Had that been why he had looked so terrible? Bloodshot eyes, grubby beard, rumpled clothing . . . Had he just collapsed into a bed in the bunkhouse to sink into an exhausted sleep when she awakened him?

A hollow feeling in the pit of her stomach told Amanda that he had. And she had accused him of being drunk! And not only that, but that it was his usual practice!

"I—yes. Yes, I believe I was," she choked because Megan seemed to be waiting for her answer. She cast a pleading look at Josh, but his unyielding gaze did nothing to relieve her.

Megan Taylor noted Amanda's agitation as well as the stiffness of her son's posture and plunged into a story about a neighbor's recent trip to Florida and Disney World. Hazel listened interestedly, but the words seemed to flow over Amanda's head. She was aware only of one thing: the man who was standing so still and watching her a short step away.

When Megan came to the end of her story, Josh moved restlessly. He bent to kiss his mother's pale cheek and reminded her that he had to see Frank before he left for town. With a short nod to Hazel and an even shorter one to Amanda, he quickly withdrew from the room.

In the following second Amanda made a decision. She mumbled an excuse—later she couldn't remember what it was—and hurried after him, unaware that Hazel's eyebrows ascended rapidly or that Megan's thin face suddenly relaxed into a small, secret smile.

Josh's long legs had carried him some distance into the yard before Amanda caught up with him. Out of breath from running, she pulled on his sleeve and held on in case he should try to move away.

He looked pointedly at her hand, then into her eyes, a cold, closed expression masking his features.

"What do you want?" he demanded impatiently, as if

he had been delayed long enough already and didn't want to waste any more time, particularly with her.

A playful breeze swirled about their legs, raising a light veil of dust; the summer sun beat down hot on their heads.

"I . . ." She had trouble finding words.

"I don't have all day, Amanda."

At his superior tone Amanda bristled. "I don't give a damn how much time you have, *Mister Taylor*! But since it's so precious . . ." She dropped her hand as if the touch of his sleeve had become repugnant and turned immediately on her heels. Only before she had taken more than one step, a long arm reached out and stopped her progress, whirling her about to face gray eyes that were shimmering with suppressed anger.

"I asked what you wanted, Amanda. I didn't stutter."

"It's not important!" Amanda retorted stubbornly.

"Probably not," he agreed, "but I'd still like to hear it."

Circumstances once again gave Amanda cause to wonder at her sanity. Earlier it had seemed so important to follow him and apologize for her behavior; but now, with the overbearing way he was acting, she realized she should have known better—known that whenever she dealt with this man she always came out the loser, whether he was foreman or wealthy ranch owner.

He gave her arm a barely restrained shake at her continued silence.

"I wanted to apologize," she blurted out resentfully, capitulating only to his superior strength, "for saying what I did!"

His eyes glittered strangely and an ugly smile began to curl the corners of his mouth.

"Having second thoughts already?" he murmured.

Confused, Amanda met his eyes. "About what?"

"Don't act stupid! You know what I mean. You've finally realized the mistake you made in turning me down, haven't you? But at the time you thought I was just a hired hand with nothing but myself to offer."

Amanda stared at him blankly. What was this man talking about? Then it dawned on her. He thought she was trying to make up to him since learning of his changed position—and changed standard of living, as if, on thinking it over, she now regretted turning down his mock proposal.

"That's not what I'm—" she began, trying to defend herself.

"You made your feelings very clear, Amanda," he interrupted shortly. "You wouldn't have me on trust because trust and empty pockets don't go together for women like you. Well, I'm sorry. But I don't give second chances. You had your opportunity and you blew it."

The sheer arrogance of that statement almost took Amanda's breath away. With smarting pride she enunciated clearly, "If you think that I would ever want to marry you, you—you're crazy! I wouldn't care if your last name was Rockefeller and you owned three fourths of the world. I'd still hate you!" Why was it that each time they met, they either tried to kill each other with words or . . . She gave her head a dismissing shake. No, she wouldn't think about that now, although one thing was for certain—with them there was no middle ground.

A slow smile relaxed his tense features as he drawled, "Is that a fact."

"Yes. I—"

"You don't hate me, Amanda," he interrupted softly.

She drew a sharp breath to continue, but it escaped her in silent sibilation as his strong fingers reached out gently to caress the side of her cheek then slowly, sensuously, trace the sensitive area around her mouth. Immediately her heart rate quickened, and she knew the truth of his words. She didn't hate him—she loved him!

Her knees almost gave way and for a second his face seemed to waver before her, but somehow she forced herself to remain upright. She loved him! This rough, arrogant, maddening, hateful, wonderful man!

He saw her moment of weakness and took full advantage of it, the touch of his lips like molten fire in her veins. But it lasted for only a second—a soft kiss that promised much more.

"You see?" he whispered, sending a shiver of pleasure down her spine. "Now tell me that you hate me."

Amanda couldn't do it. Her hands had come up to his chest during the kiss, and she knew she couldn't lie at that moment even if her life depended on it. She raised large golden eyes to his and saw the triumph he did nothing to hide.

He continued easily. "Even in out of the way places like Craigmont people know that times have changed. They're more tolerant now; they don't worry so much if a couple lives together without that little piece of paper."

Amanda became still as what he was suggesting sank into her consciousness. Had she heard him right? Had he just asked her to live with him? She searched his handsome face.

"Think about it," he instructed, his features calm. Then, after gently removing her hands, he turned and strode away, leaving her to stare after him, dumbstruck.

Amanda lay in bed that night, wide-eyed and restless, the shocking specter of his words haunting her. His mistress! He had asked her to become his mistress—or had he? Could she possibly have misunderstood? She moved her head from side to side. No. It had been a proposition all right, hinted at with just the right amount of nuance to make it cloudy, yet definitely there. How in the world had she fallen in love with such a man? But she had and now she could think of nothing else. She couldn't help but envision a life filled with him—to fall asleep in his arms each night and wake with him each morning.

The next question was, Had he meant it? Or was this just another joke to him, another test? And if it was some kind of test, why? Why was he doing it? Was he trying to humiliate her, to punish her for the honest mistake she had first made about him?

Amanda's hands curled into tight fists and pounded the sheets at her sides. How could the man suggest such a thing? And if she was fool enough to accept, did he expect to move her into the same house as his mother? Surely he wouldn't do that. He loved his mother too much to want to upset her, and from what she had seen of Megan, she would be upset. Just what was Josh attempting to do?

Somehow Amanda got through that horrible night, sleeping in snatches and cursing the day she had ever made the decision to come to the ranch.

Morning came with all the startling brightness of a midsummer day, and Amanda groaned into her pillow, her head still muzzy from lack of sleep. A shower cleared the muzziness, but did nothing for the festering ache in her heart. After breakfast she wandered aimlessly from room to room, unable to settle at anything. Finally she gave in to a sense of loneliness and called her father. Only the call refused to act as the panacea for her unease, because as she listened to his quiet voice carefully mention Carl and Marla, she found that she felt nothing. He could have been speaking of two acquaintances whose wedding was approaching. And if anything proved the validity of her newfound love, this did, for it brought home how unsubstantial her love for Carl was—that there was no comparing the two emotions. What she felt for Josh Taylor was much more overwhelming. There had been no highs and

lows with Carl—just nice steady friendship. But with Josh
. . .

The next day John Reynolds came home. He was not
expected until later in the week and Hazel was thrown into
a tizzy, scolding him for not letting her know earlier so she
could plan a big meal, and fussing about the state of the
already-spotless house. Then she bustled from the room,
muttering something about thawing some thick steaks.

John took it all in good humor and, when they were
alone, drew Amanda into a bear hug.

"And how's my favorite niece?" he asked teasingly.

"I'm fine, Uncle John," she lied. At the moment she felt
little better than an ant that had just been stepped on by
an elephant, but didn't want to tell him so.

Her uncle patted her gruffly on the back. "Love's the
very devil, isn't it?"

Startled, Amanda stiffened and pulled away. "What?"
How could he know of her feelings for Josh?

John Reynolds made a face. "Your dad called me the
other day. He told me what happened."

Relief at his knowing only the old cause of her upset
made Amanda protest weakly, "He shouldn't have."

"He thought I might be the best person to help."

His mysterious answer caused Amanda to frown; she
had always wondered why her uncle had never married.
She looked curiously into his still-handsome face.

"We'll talk about it later," he promised, then added,
"But right now, come with me. I want to show you something."

He pulled her into the room he used as his studio and
withdrew a sheaf of papers from the case he had carried
in. "What do you think?"

Amanda looked at the myriad of faces and forms that
filled the papers: people—old, young, hopeful, hopeless—

faces lined with character, alive with love, broken with despair. Her uncle had captured the very essence of human life. "Oh, Uncle John," she breathed, going through the collection again. "They're beautiful."

He didn't remark on her avid compliment but went on looking at the sketches himself. "I have a new commission, Andy. It's something a little different from what I'm used to doing"—keen blue eyes met her own—"and it's going to mean that I won't be able to be with you for more than a day or two."

Amanda let the news sink in slowly. She had hoped that her uncle's return might help keep her thoughts away from Josh, but now it seemed she would get no relief.

"Do you mind, honey?"

At his anxious inquiry Amanda hurried to reassure him. "No—no. I wouldn't dream of keeping you. What is the commission to be?"

By the time her uncle had finished telling her about the large mural that a Denver, Colorado, firm wanted painted on the lobby wall of one of its newest buildings, Amanda was almost as excited as he. The commission had come from an acquaintance who was also a devoted fan and the managing director of the firm whose company owned the building. John Reynolds had been the first and only choice for the work.

"They want it done before the place is opened to the public, so that doesn't give me much time." He named an opening date in the not too far distant future. "You can stay here as long as you like, you know—you're more than welcome to."

Amanda shook her head. The rest of the summer in Josh's company and she would be lost. No. As soon as the wedding was over, she would go home. But not just yet . . . not just yet.

\* \* \*

95

The two days of her uncle's stay at the ranch passed all too quickly for Amanda. He had looked at what little work she had completed and pronounced it well done, along with giving a few pointers on how to better it. He told her that she had natural talent and that she should develop it. But his glowing praise, which once would have lifted her spirits to the sky, did little to cheer her—especially since the sketch of Josh she had earlier removed from her pad was burning a hole in her skirt pocket. She could let no one see it, not even her uncle, but she couldn't bring herself to throw it away.

The night before he left, her uncle again broached the subject that had puzzled her so on his first day home: his reference to her father's idea that he could be of some help to her with her problem.

"It was a hard call for your father to make, Andy," her uncle began, then paused to light his pipe. "Neither of us has spoken of this for years, and I know no one else in the family knows. But, well—one time we both loved the same woman."

Amanda stared at him with her mouth slightly open.

"It was your mother." He paused to gauge the shock on her small expressive face and smiled faintly. "We're more alike than you think, Andy. Libby was just out of high school and visiting a friend of hers here—Megan Taylor, only then she was Megan White. I think you've met her." Amanda nodded her blond head quickly. "Well, to make a long story short, I fell in love with her. She seemed to like me, too, until your dad came down one week to visit me on the ranch where I was working. I introduced them."

He stopped as if he were reliving a scene from the past. "The rest is history. They got married, had you two children, then Libby died. I think your father still believes that I blame him." He puffed reflectively on his pipe. "I tried a long time ago to tell him that I didn't hold anything against him, that I would have done the same thing if our places had been reversed; but, well—he didn't seem to hear."

Amanda stared at the picture on the opposite wall. What her uncle had just told her explained so much. Why her father sometimes acted ill at ease in his brother's presence; why they had never visited the ranch.

"So you see, it took a lot of courage for him to call and tell me about Carl and Marla and you. It was like the past happening all over again."

Amanda remained quiet, absorbing everything her uncle had said. She wanted to tell him the truth, that she didn't love Carl anymore; but she knew that if she did, he would wonder why. A person didn't fall in and out of love so easily unless they found they had not been in love in the first place. And for it to have happened so suddenly could only be put to some cause—like finding another love. So she remained silent—her feelings too new, too tender, too vulnerable, to be spoken of.

Since the day at his ranch Amanda had not seen so much as a glimpse of Josh Taylor. If he was still helping to run her uncle's ranch, he seemed to be going out of his way to make sure that he avoided her.

Two days later, driven by a need that had become an almost overpowering urge, Amanda planned a visit to Megan Taylor. What Josh would make of her arrival she didn't dare think about—but she had to take the chance to see him again. Just to see him!

She dressed with more than her usual care in one of the two dresses she had brought with her. It was a soft peach color that flattered her lightly tanned skin and did much to emphasize her slender yet curving figure with its scooped neckline and tightly drawn belt. The skirt flared out over her slim hips and fell just the right length to show off her slender, shapely legs. Her makeup was light, as was her custom, but she did dip into her bag for the perfumed powder that was the same scent as her cologne. When she was done, she was happy with the picture she presented, her blond curls for once behaving as they should.

Megan Taylor was glad to see her and didn't look at all the invalid she was. After their first visit Amanda had asked Hazel just what was wrong with Megan and learned that the woman had a severe heart condition that forced her to rest much of each day. But to look at her happy carefree face, no one would believe she was impatient with her handicap.

The visit lasted only a short time, interrupted by the arrival of Mrs. James, the companion-nurse-housekeeper, whose blunt features hid a caring heart. She apologized to both of them but remained firm in the need for her charge's afternoon nap.

"But I never do anything to get tired," Megan protested, smiling.

"Then why do you drift off to sleep as soon as your head hits the pillow?" Mrs. James demanded, her hands on her ample hips.

Amanda hastened into the breach, saying that she could only stay for a few minutes anyway, and received a grateful smile from Mrs. James.

Megan Taylor pleaded softly, "I like having you visit, Amanda. Please say you'll come again."

A warm feeling descended upon Amanda. "I will," she promised. Then, with a quick smile, she moved gracefully from the room.

She was just about to step into her car when the arrival of a large brown and tan station wagon blocked her escape. She watched with quickened breath as Josh's lean form unfolded from behind the steering wheel.

98

When he came to stand in front of her, his glance took in the attractive picture she made in her peach dress, dwelling for a moment on the softly tanned skin of her throat and the beginning swell of each breast the scooped neckline revealed, before coming to rest in silent demand on her face.

Amanda reacted defensively. "I was just visiting your mother," she informed him.

He nodded. "I figured that."

"I like her."

"I figured that too." His calmness was her undoing, along with the way his gaze seemed to be riveted upon her mouth. Her heart began its usual tattoo, as one of his long arms came out to rest on her shoulder, effectively stilling any movement she might plan to make. "Sh-she had to rest," Amanda stammered.

The gray eyes suddenly clouded with what could only be a shadow of worry. "She had a bad night last night."

"Oh." Amanda swallowed, her eyes seeming to absorb his handsome features. Several long seconds passed, after which she was jerked back to awareness by his huskily worded "Don't look at me like that, Amanda."

Amanda flushed guiltily. "Like what?"

"Like you were." He took a deep, steadying breath, and Amanda knew the effect she had on him and was secretly elated.

The arm that had been resting on her shoulder moved until his fingers reached the back of her neck and began a slow, rhythmic movement, massaging the tensed muscles. Amanda could have happily collapsed at his feet.

"Have you thought about what I said?" The silver sheen in his eyes was more pronounced than usual.

Startled, her gaze flew to his, then dropped, suddenly afraid of the desire she saw there and afraid of her own response.

"Yes," she whispered.

A silent minute passed as the rhythmic movement continued.

"And?"

"Josh," she breathed achingly, swaying toward him until her forehead touched his hard chest.

He forced her chin up to look at him. "Well?"

Amanda searched his face, trying to seek out what was behind his controlled expression. "I can't, Josh."

"You like it, Amanda. You like the way I make you feel." He drew her completely against him.

Amanda fixed her eyes on the whiteness of his shirt, not wanting him to see how much she liked it, not wanting him to see the love. She loved him, but he didn't love her. On his part it was just desire, lust. Let him think that was all she felt too.

But, as always, the closeness of his body began to work on her like the most powerful of potions; the longer she remained close to his long lean form, the more disoriented she became. The only thing she knew for sure was that she didn't want to leave his warmth. She loved the feel of his skin through his shirt, the touch of his hips and hard-muscled thighs, the warm masculine scent of his body.

In her confusion she betrayed herself by saying huskily, "But your mother—" Then as realization of what she was doing crashed down upon her, she whispered tautly, achingly, "No! No, I can't. I can't do it, Josh." She looked up at him helplessly, like an animal trapped and defenseless.

The man's harsh features were expressionless.

"No second chances, Amanda," he warned.

"I don't expect any," she returned tightly.

Josh backed away and Amanda felt as if her life were over. He had offered her everything and she had rejected him—for the second time. He wouldn't ask again.

\* \* \*

The drive back to her uncle's ranch was checkered with several stops to clear the tears from her eyes and it occurred to her that all she had been doing over the past few weeks was live on the ragged edge of her emotions. Was she destined to be one of those tragic figures who would never find happiness in life? First her childish infatuation with Carl, and now the real emotion of love with Josh. She loved him—but she couldn't agree to what he wanted. She loved him too much to degrade it with what—to him—would be a casual affair. If only by some miracle he could come to love her. . . .

# CHAPTER SIX

Marla and Carl's wedding was approaching at an inordinate speed, and, as proof, Amanda received a letter from Marla asking if she would be her maid of honor. Had she been in the same frame of mind in which she left home, the letter would surely have crushed her. But now, knowing what she did about her childish infatuation for Carl, she was hardly affected. Her only worry was that Marla almost pleaded with her to come back. It was as if her sister were wondering about her hasty departure and needed to reassure herself that she had not broken Amanda's heart while listening to her own.

The noise of the small café where she was sitting hardly penetrated Amanda's consciousness, so engrossed was she in reading the letter. It was only the approach of a tall figure to the side of her table that caused her to look up.

Josh had a stack of mail held together by a rubber band in his hand showing that he, too, had gone to the small post office. Usually someone else made the trip into town to pick up her uncle's mail, but today Amanda had felt the need to come herself—the need to get away from the ranch to try to rid herself of her troubling thoughts.

"Hello, Amanda." Her heart lurched in her chest at the sound of his voice. "Mind if I sit down?"

"Would it make any difference if I did?" she countered

irritably, then promptly reburied her nose in her letter as if it contained some earth-shattering information.

"No," he replied easily, pulling out a chair and sitting down. From the corner of her eye Amanda saw him remove the band from around his mail and begin to sort through it. Young Margaret hurried over to their table, took his order for coffee, then scurried away, blushing, captivated by the spell of Josh's devastating smile.

*He should have to register that smile as a lethal weapon!* Amanda thought sourly to herself, then realized that she was jealous. She was jealous of a fourteen-year-old girl because Josh had smiled at her. How silly could a person get?

With the intention of leaving, Amanda retrieved her purse from its resting place on the table, and putting her letter into it, started to push her chair back. But the sometimes-stubborn catch on her purse delayed her as she tried to close it. When at last she won the battle and prepared to stand, her movement was stopped by a hand coming out to cover her own.

"Where do you think you're going?" Josh demanded softly.

"I'm leaving," she answered simply, evenly.

"Why?"

"You know why. Now, let me go!" She gave her hand a jerk, but he only tightened his hold. "Please!" she cried, forgetting that the café held a full morning crowd, and that heads would turn their way in curiosity.

"You do like to draw attention to yourself, don't you?" he bit out, anger making his strong jaw clamp shut. She could feel the amount of control he was putting on his temper by the tightness of his grip on her hand. Finally he let go and sat back, his pale eyes narrowing.

Amanda kept her purse in front of her as if it were a

shield that would protect her from his attractiveness. "What do you want?" she demanded.

Too late she realized the not-so-innocent interpretation he could give her words, and blushed as his tautness relaxed and his mouth turned up in an amused half smile. He replied softly, "You know what I want, Amanda. You just won't give it to me."

She looked about furtively, hoping they were not still the center of everyone's attention. Relieved, she found the people were back to their own concerns.

"Stop talking like that!" she hissed. "Don't you care what people think?"

"Not particularly," he drawled.

"Well, *I* do."

"Is that why you refused my offer? If it is, we could always go to Houston or San Antonio—anywhere where your sense of propriety won't be offended."

The fingers on her purse felt cold from holding it so tightly. Oh, she was tempted! She was more than tempted. It was all she could do not to jump at the opportunity. But she couldn't do it; instead, she took refuge in sarcasm. "Is this another chance, Josh? I thought you didn't give second chances."

He was not disturbed in the least. "Sometimes I change my mind."

"Well, I haven't." Those were the hardest words she had ever had to say.

He shrugged, the strong muscles of his shoulders moving under the blue cotton of his shirt. Margaret came to the table to serve his coffee and was promptly directed to refill Amanda's empty cup even though she tried to refuse. When the girl had gone, Amanda flashed, "Do you always like to be the big boss, Josh? Does it give you some kind of special thrill?"

He ignored her, gathering together his letters, replacing

the rubber band, then moving them to a position beside his cup. Amanda relaxed slightly as his attention left her for a moment. She relinquished the death grip on her purse and slid it onto her lap.

The silence between them lasted until their coffee was almost finished. Then he surprised her by asking casually, "That letter you were reading—was it anything important?"

Indignantly Amanda replied, "I don't think that's any of your business!"

"From the old boyfriend?" he persisted.

Startled, Amanda looked up. "What do you mean?"

"The boyfriend. The one who's going to marry your sister."

Aghast that he knew, Amanda had to forcibly stop herself from screaming. Instead, she demanded icily, "How did you find out about that?"

"You come from a small town, Amanda," he replied easily. "You know how everyone always knows everyone else's business." He struck a match to light a cigarette.

"But that's impossible! I'm not *from* here. No one—"

"Your uncle knows."

"He didn't tell you—he wouldn't!" At that moment, if what Josh was intimating was true, her anger was divided equally between the two men. And where else would he have got the information if not from her uncle?

"I'm the only one he told, so don't worry. And he only told me because he wanted me to try to help keep your spirits up."

Keep her spirits up. If only her uncle knew! Josh watched her from behind a cloud of smoke as she tried valiantly to pull herself together.

After achieving some measure of success, she shakily retorted, "My spirits are just fine, thank you. I'll relieve you of the duty."

"I didn't say I accepted. I just said he asked."

The astringency of his reply effectively cut off any further protest.

"Now, tell me about the letter."

Amanda slumped back in her chair, suddenly tired of their constant fighting. "It's from my sister."

"The one who's getting married?"

"Yes, I have only one."

"Wedding still on?"

Amanda nodded.

"Are you going to go?"

"I have to," she replied simply. "She wants me to be the maid of honor."

He whistled softly. "Does she know how you feel?"

It was something of a relief to have him think she loved someone else. Maybe now that he did, he would leave her alone.

"Of course not. I've convinced her I don't love Carl."

He exhaled another cloud of smoke. "You must be a pretty good little actress."

*And you don't know the half of it!* she thought wretchedly.

"When is this wedding going to take place?"

Amanda was more than beginning to resent this unwarranted prying into her private business. "A week from tomorrow . . . as if you care," she retorted crisply.

He smiled slightly at her returning spirit, then made a show of crushing out his cigarette in the battered tin ashtray on the table. "Is it going to be a large wedding?"

"That depends on what you mean by large," she answered sweetly. "Not anything like the great Josh Taylor's will be when he finally gets caught, but it will be big enough. Most of the town is coming."

He watched her narrowly for another long moment, and Amanda shifted restlessly. Then he astonished her by saying, "I think it might be a good idea if I came with you."

"You *what*?" she squeaked when she could find her voice.

"I'm coming with you."

"But why?" she asked incredulously.

"Your uncle asked me to look after you, and I take my promises seriously. Look"—he sat forward until his arms were resting, crossed, on the wooden table—"I saw the way you worried over that letter. You don't want anyone in that town, especially your sister, to think you're still pining after—whatever-his-name-is—so the best solution is to bring along a boyfriend of your own. If anything will put a stop to all the speculation, that will."

Amanda fixed amazed tawny eyes on his lean form. He had hit the root of her problem and come up with an answer. She *was* concerned about Marla—about what more she could do to convince her she now truly didn't care. As for the townspeople, the only reason she worried about them at all was because it might put a blight on the wedding to have people speculating. And until that astounding offer came from the man across from her, she didn't have any idea of how she was going to handle the situation. Only could she let him do it? Wouldn't it be exchanging one set of problems for another by having Josh accompany her, acting as her special friend in order to relieve her family's minds and take the townspeople's thoughts off the possible tenderness of her feelings? It was all a little mind-boggling.

"But—"

"I've told you before, no buts."

Amanda stared down at her tightly clasped hands, not really seeing them. What would he do if she told him the truth? That she didn't feel anything for Carl anymore other than a sense of sisterly affection? Would he believe

108

her? And did she want him to know? Of course not. If he knew, he might try to convince her to change her mind again. And the third time might prove fatal. But then again, living in such close contact with him for the several days it would take to attend the wedding might prove fatal in itself. Her hands began to tremble slightly and she pressed them together even tighter.

"No . . . I don't think it would be a good idea." Unconsciously she firmed her chin.

"Why?" he challenged softly. "Are you afraid?"

Because that was precisely what she was, Amanda circled her dry lips with her tongue. He always seemed able to touch her sore spot.

"Think about it, Amanda," he continued. "If you ever plan to go back to that town to live, you'll have to put up with all the pitying glances and the whispers. Oh, people won't do it to be mean; you'll just be a distraction in their otherwise ordinary lives. You'll be poor Amanda—jilted for her own sister! And memories live long. Especially in small towns."

Amanda dropped her eyes, her nerves in a jumble. What he said was true—Megan still remembered her uncle's loss. Probably others did too.

"Think about it," he said. "And then think about how it would be if I came along. No pity. Speculation turned from you to me. And"—his voice dropped to a soft intimate tone—"no one but the two of us will know that it's all totally unnecessary."

Suddenly afraid, Amanda whispered. "What do you mean?"

"That you don't love him and that you never did."

Amanda felt trapped. He had guessed! "I did!" she cried intensely. "I do!" Tears were coming into her eyes, and she had to blink to keep them back, too caught up in emotion to see that once again they were the objects of interested glances. If she admitted to him that he was right, it would be like telling him that she loved him. And that she could never do. She would be lost if he ever learned. It would be the final lever he would use against her and she knew she would crumble.

Trying desperately to get his mind off what he had said, she went back to his original subject. "But if you come with me, people will think—"

He shrugged carelessly. "So what?"

"Wouldn't it bother you? All the talk? All the sly looks and the questions? They'll have us engaged before the cake is cut!"

His eyes met hers steadily across the table, and she could not look away. "Let them. We'll know where we stand."

"Aren't you afraid I might hold you to it?" she challenged, trying to break his calm.

"I don't do anything I don't want to do, Amanda." The words were spoken softly, but she heard the implied threat and looked away.

"All right," she whispered. "You win. You can come. I'll let my sister know I'm bringing a guest."

With that she rose to her feet and this time there was no outthrust hand to halt her progress. All the same she paused to interject one more thought. "But I don't like it."

His smile was taunting as his silver eyes ran boldly over the intimate curves of her body, dwelling for a moment on her shapely legs and slim hips before moving on to her rounded breasts. It was as if he were mentally undressing her and touching what he found! Amanda's heart raced in response to the desire she saw kindle deep within the gray depths. He wanted her. And she wanted him. But there was a world of difference in their need: hers involved love and tenderness; his was purely a basic response to the clamor of masculine hormones.

The clatter of dishes being removed from a nearby table broke the tension between them, and with an incoherent murmur Amanda pushed past the young waitress to almost run out of the café.

The memory of the raw sexual excitement his look had aroused made Amanda tremendously restless for the next few days. She knew the trip was a mistake but was helpless to do anything about it. She had already called Marla to break the news, and her sister had sounded so happy and relieved that there was no way she could call back now and say that it had all been a huge mistake. Marla had gone on to tell her about the bridal gown a neighbor had sewed and of the color of the material for the maid of honor's dress she had chosen with Amanda in mind and that she was waiting for her consent before having it made. The conversation had run well over an hour. At the end Amanda felt emotionally drained.

It was with a great sense of fatalism that she sent a message to Josh the next day asking if he would be able to leave Friday morning. The wedding was to take place Saturday, but the rehearsal was set for the night before. Marla had insisted that she come for it and bring Josh with her—that there would be plenty of room for him in the house, as most of their relatives were coming from their own homes in the Dallas/Fort Worth area.

An answer was sent back almost immediately. In a firm dark hand, Josh accepted, telling her he would pick her up. That and nothing more.

Amanda folded the note and put it in the same drawer in which she had placed the drawing.

## CHAPTER SEVEN

The sun rose Friday morning much sooner than Amanda was prepared for. Somehow her alarm clock, which had never let her down before, failed to go off, and even the roosters seemed to be on strike. As a result she had to jump into the shower and almost throw on her clothing. Josh had said he would be there by seven, and she didn't want to give him an excuse to taunt her with her lateness.

She was in the kitchen, making an attempt to swallow scalding hot coffee and listening to an aggrieved tirade from Hazel about the importance of eating a proper breakfast, when she heard a car approaching.

Hurriedly she put down her still-half-filled cup and moved to the window, pulling the curtain aside in order to see better. It was the station wagon, and Josh was slowly unfolding his length from its interior. The curtain fluttered back into place as soon as he started up the walkway, but she continued to watch. He was dressed in dark chocolate-brown Levi's jeans with a matching jacket and an earth-tone patterned shirt. His springy dark hair was brushed back from his forehead, but Amanda knew it would soon return to its natural position. The rugged planes of his tanned face were forever etched in her heart, and she longed to run to him; to feel the hard strength of his body; to smooth her hands over his chest and shoulders; to feel the play of muscle as he strained her close; to kiss him until they both forgot time and place. . . . But she did not. She could not allow herself to give in to her desires. By the time he knocked on the door she was back in her seat at the table, outwardly composed and taking another sip of the too-hot coffee.

His smile was easy as his gaze ran over her from the tumble of blond curls to her pale blue blouse and white jeans. "Morning," he greeted her, then turned to include Hazel in the greeting.

"Good morning, Josh," Hazel repeated, already reaching into a cabinet. "Would you like a cup of coffee before you start?"

"No, but thanks, Hazel. Amanda and I have a long way to go, so I think it would be better if we got started right away."

Amanda lowered her cup with a small clatter and pushed to her feet.

Hazel grunted and began to thump her hearing aid. "Oh, it's no use! I could hear only about half of what you said, Josh. Something goes wrong with this thing every time I turn around!"

Josh walked over and put a long arm around the woman's narrow shoulders. He hugged her for a moment, then said close to her face: "I said, no, but thanks, Hazel. We have to go." He released his hold. "Get one of the boys to take you into town today. You need to get that hearing aid checked out."

Hazel, who usually didn't like to be told what to do, nodded cooperatively. "All right, Josh. I will."

Josh turned to Amanda, who had silently watched the small scene. "Ready?"

"Of course," she replied, reaching for her purse and small overnight bag. Earlier she had decided it was silly to bring many changes of clothing with her. Everything she would need could be found in her home. She had more clothes there than at the ranch. She surprised Hazel with a quick kiss on her cheek before hurrying from the room. Seeing Josh act so caringly toward the older woman had made it suddenly difficult for her to breathe. It seemed he was capable of tenderness, but carefully reserved it for women over the age of fifty!

Josh caught up with her at the door to the car. He looked down into her small tight face curiously and raised an inquiring brow. "Anxious to see the boyfriend?"

Amanda opened the door and got in without replying.

Neither exerted the effort to make brilliant conversation for the next hundred miles. Only an occasional word passed between them, and soon Amanda felt overwhelmingly sleepy. She had not slept well last night, anticipating what the next few days would bring, so that the drone of the car's engine, coupled with the silence and mile upon mile of interstate highway, soon had their effect.

She felt her eyelids grow increasingly heavy and repeatedly jerked them open, but soon their weight was more than she could deal with and in the end she gave up the effort.

She came back to awareness sometime later, with her head lying against something solid yet strangely yielding. She felt the warmth and smiled a sleep-induced contented smile, her half-awakened mind content to find that the pleasant dream she had been having had not come to an end. She turned her cheek closer into the cloth covering Josh's shoulder. She could feel the muscles of his arm move as he directed the course of the car and she could see the steady rise and fall of his chest as he breathed. Suddenly she became very still, her now-wide-awake mind realizing just where she was. But she did not pull away; she remained there, silently enjoying the stolen moments of closeness.

115

Her cheek was pressed against his upper arm and several blond curls were spread out against the dark material of his jacket. Then she became aware that one of her hands was resting on the hard muscle of his thigh and it was all she could do not to draw in a startled breath. For where only a moment before the hand had rested in perfect innocence, it now suddenly seemed to catch fire. She knew she should move it but couldn't.

Several long, tortuous miles flew by and it was becoming increasingly hard for her to pretend to be asleep. Her body cried out for one thing and her mind screamed the opposite.

Unexpectedly a large hand left the steering wheel, covered her own where it rested on his thigh, and pressed it down even harder against him.

"Amanda?" The deep voice was low and husky.

Amanda froze, for the first time noticing that his breathing had quickened and that the car had seemed to decrease in speed. She sat up with a jerk, snatching her hand away.

"W-what is it?" she asked, her voice trembling as she tried to pretend she had just awakened.

Narrowed gray eyes searched her flushed face, and noting the inability of her eyes to hold his, he replied steadily, "I think you know."

"I was asleep," she lied.

"Like hell you were!"

"I was!"

"Sure, earlier." He attempted to catch the hand that had been resting against him, but Amanda drew it back as if from a flame. He laughed shortly at her revealing action. "See?"

Amanda said nothing but scooted toward the far side of the seat to pointedly look outside.

Josh watched her estimatingly for several seconds, then

asked tauntingly, "What do you keep running away from, honey? Me? Or yourself?"

Amanda stayed awake and silent for the rest of the long trip. She could feel no gladness when the terrain became more familiar as they approached the town where she had grown up. She could feel nothing but an almost primitive sense of panic. Josh was right. It was herself she was running away from. And they both knew it.

The town of Kemperville was a little larger than Craigmont. It had a theater and a roller-skating rink and even boasted a volunteer fire department. The town's proximity to Dallas probably accounted for its recent prosperity, even though it still retained a small-town flavor in its look—and in the minds of its citizens. The large interstate highway, only a few miles away, easily made the farming community a short drive to its giant neighbor.

Following her quietly worded directions, Josh guided the car to her family's home. It was a neat wooden building that had been painted white with green trimming. She saw Josh's narrow glance go over the house and the few acres that surrounded it; in no way did he let his thoughts as to its comparison with his own gigantic ranch be seen.

Almost before the car had come to a stop, people were emerging from the front door and hurrying down the veranda steps and out to the circular drive. As soon as Amanda stepped out of the car, Marla launched herself at her. And two cousins she had not seen in years stood to one side, waiting until she had been freed before they too each gave her an affectionate hug.

A bit overwhelmed by the greeting, Amanda was still able to see the effect Josh had on the women as he came around from the driver's side of the car. One cousin began to run a hand over her long brown hair and the other just stared at him wide-eyed and with her mouth slightly opened in surprise. Amanda could sympathize with them both—Josh just seemed to exude virility.

Marla, when she finally pulled her eyes from her sister, looked with even wider blue eyes toward the stranger.

"Marla, everyone. This is Josh Taylor." Amanda couldn't help the note of pride that entered her voice as she introduced him. After all, he was the man she loved, even if he didn't love her, and she was presenting him to her family.

Josh smiled his devastating smile and ran his silver eyes over each female present, but his last look was for Amanda. She tried to interpret that long, mocking yet surprisingly tender smile but couldn't.

"Which one is Marla?" he asked, flicking his gaze once again over the women, a smile crinkling the skin at the corners of his eyes and deepening the creases in his cheeks.

Marla jumped as if on a string. "I am."

Josh nodded. "I should have known. Thank you for letting me come to your wedding." He reached out and drew a startled Amanda close to his side. "I couldn't let this one get too far away from me. She might have decided not to come back."

An embarrassed yet intrigued laugh rose up from the group at his frank words, and Amanda felt her face flame. If only she could believe that! But he was a man who liked to tease—often at her expense, as well she knew—and since he had taken it upon himself to write his own part, he was now going to play it to the hilt. She could take nothing he said seriously their entire time here.

She stiffened slightly and his arm fell away. "Where's Daddy?" she asked of anyone not too bemused to answer.

The spell broke first for Marla. "He's inside." A twinkle entered her eyes. "He said he would wait until the rush was over."

Amanda had thought about the meeting between the

two men she cared most for in her life, wondering how they would react to each other, but she should have known that she would have nothing to worry about.

Her father was standing in the middle of the small living room, his still-attractive features showing proudly the marks of time and care, his mane of silver hair combed smoothly into place.

At first the two men just looked at each other and Amanda, who was attuned to each, knew the instant appraisal that was being made—the quick assessment of the other's character, the decision about whether to like or dislike. She gave an inaudible sigh of relief when each man reached out his right hand at the same moment to clasp the other's in friendly greeting. She felt ridiculously happy. Her father had a way of rating people according to his first impression, and she realized now she should have known that he would like Josh: Josh had the kind of strength her father admired.

Marla and the two cousins who had followed her into the kitchen in order to help prepare refreshments came back into the room, Marla carrying a large tray.

"Aunt Margaret is with Aunt Eileen, Amanda." Marla passed a glass filled with lemonade to her, naming their father's younger sister. "They've gone over to Mrs. Beck's for a little gossip." She turned to Josh, who was now standing at his ease by her father. "I suppose Amanda has told you all about Aunt Margaret."

"Some," Josh answered, and directed a look at Amanda, who had sunk into a familiar overstuffed chair.

Marla continued to pass around glasses and then offered a plate of her aunt's delicious chocolate nut cookies. Each man took a cookie but held his untasted glass in such a manner as to suggest that it contained something noxious.

Marla, her duty done, came to sit in the matching chair across from Amanda. She turned impish blue eyes on the man standing across from her. "Josh, if you'll let Amanda out of your sight for a few seconds later on, I'd like to show her my wedding dress. I promise I'll bring her back."

All eyes were on Amanda, especially her father's.

"I think I might be persuaded to," Josh answered drolly, and only Amanda heard the taunt. She shot him a quelling glance that he ignored.

"Good, then we'll go after we finish our drinks. And," Marla said, turning to Amanda, "you have to see what you're going to wear. It's absolutely gorgeous!"

Amanda smiled at her sister's enthusiasm although her eyes remained with the two men. Her father was about to put the glass to his lips but brought it down in disgust.

"Lemonade! I can't *stand* the stuff!" His eyes met Josh's, and they both seemed to agree silently.

Her father put his glass down on the coffee table and took Josh's unprotestingly from his hand. "Nothing against you girls," Patrick Reynolds quickly noted, "but I've developed an aversion to lemonade over the years."

"But, Daddy," Marla teased, her face lighting up with suppressed laughter, "Aunt Margaret made it especially for you. You know how she feels about social drinking— even at weddings. She's made so much lemonade, the refrigerator is positively afloat with it. You *have* to help us drink it!"

Patrick Reynolds fixed his younger daughter with an irascible eye. "Look, my girl. You're going to be a bride tomorrow. But if I keep drinking this stuff, I don't know if I'll live to walk you down the aisle!" Marla began to giggle. "Come on, son, I think I know where to find something a little more to our taste. Amanda, Marla. We'll be in my study if anyone wants to know. And we don't want to be disturbed."

Amanda's reply was choked off by her sister's laughing

120

warning. "You'd better close the curtains, Dad. Aunt Margaret might sneak up on you."

Patrick Reynolds left the room muttering something about the fact that a man's home was supposed to be his castle, and he was followed by an amused Josh, who paused long enough beside Amanda's chair to reach out and gently caress her cheek with one long finger in total disregard of three pairs of interested eyes. He let it drop slowly away, then was gone.

Even before she could still the clamor that his touch had set off, her sister and her cousins descended upon her, exclaiming how absolutely gorgeous they thought Josh was, and asking how she had met him, how serious it was between them, and just about anything she would allow them to ask.

It took several seconds for her to pull herself together enough to give answers that would satisfy them and yet tell nothing. Somehow she succeeded, because several minutes later Marla could contain herself no longer and insisted that Amanda come look at her dress.

The wedding gown had the place of honor in her sister's closet. Lovingly Marla brought it out and removed the plastic covering that kept away not only dust and dirt but the repeated, dreamily fingered touchings of the bride-to-be, who liked to look at it each time she came into her room.

"Well, what do you think?" she asked proudly, already knowing the answer.

"It's beautiful, absolutely beautiful," Amanda breathed sincerely. The dress was a soft ivory satin with thousands of tiny seed pearls lovingly stitched along the bodice and hem. It was an Empire-style dress and had a moderately long train that would look positively stunning on Marla.

Marla reverently brought out the delicate veil.

"Beautiful," Amanda repeated. She turned to smile at her two cousins, who smiled back in return.

Marla then directed Amanda's attention to the array of wedding gifts that were, for the moment, sitting on the bed. Marla had almost everything a young bride would need to set up housekeeping, and Amanda wondered what was left for her to give. She had been too wrapped up in herself and her problems to think of anything appropriate. She would have to give the matter some thought. They spent a pleasant half hour going through all the beautiful things, then, as the two cousins were closely examining an antique lace tablecloth, Marla drew Amanda quietly aside.

"It—it is okay, isn't it, Amanda?"

The shadowed blue eyes pleaded with her to tell the truth, and for a moment Amanda was impatient with her younger sister. Just what did she expect her to say? Cancel the wedding? Then her face softened, and she replied honestly, "Of course, it is. Carl's like a brother to me, and tomorrow he really will become one." She kissed her sister's cheek. "I hope you'll be very happy, Marla."

The sincerity of her voice, along with the memory of the lean, powerful man who was at that moment in the study with their father, convinced Marla totally. Impulsively she hugged Amanda, almost crushing the very life out of her. "I thought that was how it was, but—well, I started to wonder. Oh, thank you, Amanda, thank you."

Laughing, Amanda disengaged herself from her sister's tight hold. She had told the truth, but if it hadn't been for Josh's unforgettable presence, she knew she would have had much more difficulty. As it was, Marla did believe her, and that solved one of her greatest worries.

The wedding rehearsal went off perfectly, the minister

of the small congregation giving last-minute instructions and assuring a very nervous Carl that all would be well.

Afterward there was a rehearsal dinner at Carl's home, prepared by his mother and her family. It was a large, happy affair with people filling the small house to overflowing, causing some of the guests to sit on the front porch and some to even spill out onto the lawn.

Amanda and Josh soon found themselves on the porch pushed up against the unoccupied porch swing, so that they wordlessly agreed to use it.

"Phew!" Josh said, settling his long frame. "A lot of work goes into getting married."

Amanda smiled and began to reply, but a nearby uncle of Carl's overheard and interrupted, laughing. "It's been the cause of many an elopement, I can tell you. I did it myself twenty years ago and can't say that I'd do it any different today. My wife would, though. Look at her." He directed their attention to a plump matronly woman dressed in a tight pink dress with her hair pulled slickly back into a high chignon. "Loves every minute of this. And drags me to every wedding around—for revenge, I think," he added darkly, but there was a tender look in his eye as he watched his wife's face that belied his statement.

Josh laughed in fellow feeling, then, as the man turned and began talking to someone else, he placed a finger under Amanda's chin and asked quietly, "Do you want to fight that crowd again or would you like me to get something for us to eat?"

A rash of shivers ran over Amanda at the intimate way he was leaning toward her. "No—you do it, Josh."

Something flashed in the depths of his eyes and momentarily made her heart beat out of sync, but whatever it was, it was soon replaced by the tolerant humor that had so far marked his behavior toward her during the last few hours.

Amanda was tired, and it showed in her face when Josh

was no longer present. It was as if the spark that had kept her going had suddenly disappeared, and she was lost without it. Sighing deeply, she folded her arms across her waist and closed her eyes, appreciating the gentle night breeze that sometimes made its way through the crowd and brushed across her face. She would be glad when all of this was over—glad when the pretense could end. She liked the feeling of having Josh be attentive to her, being near whenever the need arose. It could become habit-forming—and she must not let that happen. When this was over they would return to their state of armed attraction, each waiting for the other to break, with only her knowing that what she wanted from him he would find impossible to give.

She felt the swing bounce as someone sat down on it and she looked up quickly. Not enough time had passed for Josh to have returned.

The newcomer was Carl. His brown eyes were a little glassy and his words slurred slightly as he spoke. "Hello, Andy, long time no see!"

"Carl." This was the first time Amanda had spoken to Carl since returning to Kemperville. In church he had nodded an abstracted "Hello" before having his attention called away.

"What are you doing here by yourself? Where's that man I saw you with earlier?"

Carl tried to cross his legs, but the top one kept insisting on falling off. Finally he gave up and steadied his knees with his elbows. Obviously he had been doing a little too much celebrating.

"He went to get us something to eat," Amanda replied, a small smile forming on her lips. Carl was not the sort to indulge in drinking bouts. His mother had the same view as Aunt Margaret as to the evils of drink, so some of his friends, whom Amanda had seen earlier bunched around the prospective bridegroom, must have thought it good fun to sneak in some hard liquor—and give most of it to Carl!

"I—I got to do that too. Haven't had much to eat all day." He smiled happily to himself. ". . . a little too much to drink though. Some of the guys came by to say hello."

"I had that feeling," Amanda murmured, a wave of maternal emotion swamping her. Really, he was just like a little boy. How could she ever have thought she loved him enough to marry him? Oh, she loved him—but it was just as she had told Marla earlier: as if he were her brother. They had been close for so long; they had played with each other since childhood. Carl was handsome in a Teutonic sort of way: big and blond, with huge muscular shoulders and strength he didn't even know he possessed. But emotionally, as she had noticed only this evening, he had a long way to go before he had the calm assurance that Josh seemed to have been born with.

Thinking of Josh seemed to conjure him up. She saw his quick frown as he took in the sight of the two of them sitting on the swing, Carl now leaning back lazily with one arm thrown negligently along the back of the swing, in effect encircling Amanda's slender shoulders. When Josh came to a stop before them, two filled plates in his hands, an even deeper frown was darkening his brow.

"Am I interrupting anything?" His voice was ice-cold as he looked disparagingly from Carl to Amanda.

Amanda jerked forward as if caught in a guilty act. "No—nothing!" she denied almost too quickly, and felt her cheeks burn under his narrowing look.

Carl tried to get up, but it took two attempts. "Say— what's your name? I don't think we've been intro—intro —introduced," he got out proudly, and unsteadily extended his hand.

"Carl, this is Josh Taylor," Amanda said quickly, see-

125

ing the way Josh's jaw had clamped more tightly shut with each slurred word that Carl uttered.

"Josh—good to meet you." Carl's aim was off, and he nearly toppled forward as he tried to shake hands. Somehow he regained his balance, but it was only for a second as he immediately sank back onto the swing.

In a voice that brooked no disobedience Josh instructed, "I think you better find Marla, Amanda. I'll keep our friend here company until you get back. That is, unless you'd rather stay with your boyfriend and have me go find her."

If it weren't for the shocked looks that the incident would arouse—and attention, Amanda thought, was definitely something to be avoided right now—she would happily have pushed Josh right off the porch. He made her so angry!

"He's not my boyfriend!" she snapped from between clenched teeth.

"But he was." It was said quietly and with just that little bit of edge that made its meaning clear. Josh was wondering what she had ever seen in Carl; since she had just been wondering that very thing herself, it only added to her anger. It was everything she could do to turn away from those hard, mocking eyes and go in search of her sister.

Marla was not hard to find in the crowd, her happy girlish laughter leading Amanda to her. With only a little difficulty she made her way inside the group and whispered in her sister's ear. Marla frowned and nodded assent, then after making excuses to her friends followed Amanda to the porch. Marla sighed when she saw the too relaxed form that Josh's broad back was shielding from view of the others in the area.

Carl looked up, and a beautiful light spread over his inebriated face. "Marla, honey, I was looking all over for you." He tried to reach out and grasp her but missed.

"Sure you were," Marla replied, her humor restored at the sight of the momentarily confused look in Carl's eyes when his hands came back empty. "Come on." She took hold of one of his brawny arms and began to pull. "I think we better hide you before Aunt Margaret sees you. You'll spend years trying to get back into her good graces if she catches you like this."

Her strength was nothing in comparison to Carl's massive bulk, which had suddenly seemed to lose the ability to stand. Marla cast an appealing glance toward Josh. "Do you think you could help me get him out to the car? And Amanda, if you could bring one of those plates and find some strong coffee . . ." She motioned toward the two full plates that Josh had balanced on the porch railing.

"Of course," Amanda agreed at once.

In one easy movement Josh had Carl on his feet. Amanda watched their progress as they made their way down the steps. She sighed with relief: no one seemed to notice that one of the three was almost being carried.

The car Marla had guided Josh to was on the far side of the garage and turned away from the house. It was only the light of the moon that showed Amanda the path as she hurried toward them, both of her hands full, guided by the sound of their voices.

"Is there anything else we can do, Marla?" she asked breathlessly, still recovering from her hurried walk from the house. She put the cup and plate on the car's front fender.

"No, I don't think so." Marla looked down at Carl's blond head, which was bent close to his chest as he sat sideways in the passenger side of the front seat. "I think all he needs is some food and time. I could just shoot those so-called friends of his!"

"Some people would say that every man has the right to get a little smashed on the eve of his wedding." Josh's soft voice broke into the stillness. "Men don't give up their freedom very easily."

"And women do?" Amanda bridled, resenting his suggestion.

"No, I didn't say that. Some are more stubborn than others and require a little persuasion."

Amanda could find no reply. He seemed to be talking in circles. Instead, she contented herself with a furious glare and an impotent clenching of her fists.

"I think he'll be okay now," Josh pronounced. "After a little bit you might try some of that coffee."

"I will. Thank you, Josh." Marla didn't take her eyes away from her fiancé. "Thanks, Amanda."

Amanda mumbled a reply and soon found her arm taken in a grip that left her no option but to follow. Josh didn't go back toward the house but farther out into the backyard. They walked on silently for several minutes, until the sounds of the gathering could no longer be heard.

Josh stopped beneath the low, sheltering branches of a large tree and turned her toward him, the leaf-filtered light from the moon above showing that his eyes were glittering strangely. Without saying a word, the fingers of his free hand came up to spread against her back, drawing her close as his mouth lowered to hers.

Once again his kiss began roughly, as if somehow he were trying to mark her as his possession, but after the first few seconds, the tenor slowly changed into a sensual assault that had Amanda winding her arms around his neck trying to draw him even nearer. His lips left her mouth to blaze a trail of fire down the side of her neck, lingering for a moment on the hollow of her throat where the tip of his tongue tasted the silken softness of her skin, and caused quicksilver flames to shoot through Amanda's limbs.

She heard him breathe her name disjointedly and knew that in that moment, he was as much a prisoner of his passion as she was of hers. Wordlessly Josh drew her down to the cool grass, kneeling for a moment over her before lowering his long form. Once more he sought out her lips with the searing touch of his own, making Amanda ache deep inside with a desire to be even closer. Pressed into the firm, damp earth, the pressure of his weight seemed a precious burden to her and her arms rose up to encircle his waist, her hands caressing the muscular contours of his broad shoulders and back with a touch that cherished. She longed to explore every inch of him, to give this man that she so loved and wanted as much pleasure as she possibly could. With urgent fingers he began tugging aside the thin shoulder straps of her dress and, when he had succeeded, drew away the remainder of the bodice. Gently he caressed the rounded breasts that gleamed white in the moonlight and Amanda felt them swell in response. She groaned aloud when his head bent to follow his seeking hands and his teasing tongue rubbed against the ever-hardening rosy tips. Never had Amanda experienced such a burning delight; she was transported to another world, a world she never wanted to leave.

Josh shifted, trapping one of her legs beneath his and Amanda found herself responding with total abandon to the insistent pressure of his thigh between hers. Her breath was ragged, her entire being consumed with a sudden fire as she arched herself up against him, her fingers tangling in his thick, dark hair. Her uninhibited response seemed to raise Josh's passion to even greater heights and Amanda felt him shudder against her as he murmured her name against her breast. With an overwhelming sense of certainty, Amanda knew that it was right, that she was meant to soar to the very heights of passion in the arms of Josh Taylor, that he was some missing part of her, half of a wholeness her soul hungered to be joined with—if only for a fiery moment.

Josh's heart was thundering as his mouth moved to fasten once again on her own and her fingers, of their own volition, began a frantic loosening of the buttons of the shirt that was keeping their flesh apart. More than ever, Amanda needed to be joined with him as one, to feel that strong body pressed closely against her own in complete union. Josh began to tremble as her fingers trailed through the fine growth of hair that covered his chest, and lower, to his taut, warm abdomen. Guided by instinct alone, her hands dropped to his belt. She felt him stiffen, heard the ragged edge to each breath he drew . . . Then suddenly she was being thrust away, his fingers unknowingly digging into the flesh of her upper arms.

"God, woman," he said, his voice shaken. "We have to stop. If we don't, I'll take you right here."

Slowly, unwillingly, Amanda came back to awareness, but her golden eyes still shone with her aroused emotions; Josh looked at her as if it were all he could do not to pull her back into his arms.

"Stop it, Amanda," he ordered huskily, giving her shoulders a short shake.

That action was what it took. With flushing cheeks and tears of frustration blurring her eyes, Amanda tried to cover herself.

"God, you're beautiful," he breathed, a little of his strictly enforced control breaking as he watched her movements.

"Don't," she begged, realizing at last how perilously close she had come to catastrophe.

His gray eyes were on her face as she finished readjusting her dress and remained unblinking while she stood up and ran trembling fingers through her blond curls. She couldn't look at him. All the many times he had kissed her she had responded, but never to such a degree. She had never felt quite so shaken. He came to his feet beside her.

She began to turn away but was halted by Josh's fingers gripping her forearm. Reluctantly she raised her eyes.

A muscle was working in the strong line of his jaw and his face had become curiously harsh, but desire still glittered in the silver depths of his gaze as he grated roughly, "You're mine, Amanda. No one else's. You belong to *me*!"

Thrown more than a little off balance by the intensity of his words, Amanda could only stare at him. She felt something like a marionette waiting for the puppeteer to pull its strings.

As long seconds passed and she still made no reply—she just continued to look at him blankly—Josh uttered a smothered curse and spun her about, forcing her to move with him.

When they neared the house, Amanda automatically turned toward it, but Josh bit out curtly, "We're leaving," and she found that she didn't have the will to argue. She didn't want to face anyone now. What was it she had read once about the fact that people could tell when a woman had been thoroughly kissed? Well, she had been—more than thoroughly—and all she wanted to do was find somewhere quiet to hide and lick her wounds.

What would it matter that people would miss them and talk about their early departure? That was what this whole thing was about, wasn't it?

But, sick at heart, Amanda knew that it was not.

## CHAPTER EIGHT

Exhausted both physically and mentally, Amanda slept late the next morning. When she finally awakened, she had to make herself get out of bed. Then, after showering and dressing in a cool cotton print dress, she wanted only to find the kitchen and some hot coffee, forgetting for the moment just what day it was. But she was not to remain ignorant for long: the house was a beehive of activity. And the fact that she had slept through all the happy laughter and mingling of voices as they came from different rooms proved without a doubt the depth of her exhaustion.

Marla was in her bedroom laughing excitedly with their cousins, and Amanda had to pass carefully to avoid being brought into the cheerful preparations. It wasn't that she didn't want to be with her sister on her happiest day, it was just that she couldn't face so much joy so early, especially after last night.

Making her way downstairs, Amanda heard voices coming from the living room and realized that this was where her Aunt Margaret was holding court. The voices were more mature, the laughter more sedate, and it was definitely an all-female gathering. Where her father and Josh and the rest of the men were, she had no idea; but mercifully the kitchen proved to be empty, and Amanda gave a heartfelt sigh of relief. She put on the kettle and sank down into a chair at the table, her hands supporting

133

her dully aching head, a legacy of the disturbed night she had spent.

The short trip home last night had been filled with a tense silence—as if neither she nor Josh were willing to break it. They had parted stiffly after Amanda stood fumbling with the front door key so badly that Josh had to take it away from her and insert it himself. She had kept her gaze firmly on the faded carpeting while he switched on the lights and, after mumbling a hasty good-night, fled upstairs.

Immediately she had undressed and climbed between the sheets but had not gone directly to sleep. She had stared with wide eyes into the darkness, hearing the restless movements that came from the room down the hall, reliving the few precious moments of ecstasy that had been spent under the protective limbs of the tree, and fighting the knowledge that she had only to take a few steps down the hall for that mindless rapture to reach fulfillment.

Her agonizing situation had not been helped a great deal by the arrival later of the rest of her family. She had lain awake listening to them as they talked and went about the business of preparing for bed. Finally, as the old house settled into a quietness that signaled the rest of its occupants' sleepiness, Amanda crawled out of bed and slowly walked over to the window. The night air had been cool; she had stared out into it for some time before she became aware of a flicker of light that arced in the distance. Hastily she had taken a step back; then, realizing it would be impossible for her to be seen from below as her bedroom was still in darkness, she watched, barely breathing, as a long lean familiar figure came down the walkway from the road to pause and slowly crush a cigarette underfoot. The moonlight revealed his rugged features, and Amanda felt her heart begin to beat steadily faster. She watched as he started to walk forward again. Soon the door clicked below as he entered and locked it. She honestly didn't know if she was relieved or disappointed when he passed her room without hesitation and shut the door to his own.

The insistent whistling of the kettle made her raise her head and rub the back of her neck, trying to relieve some of the tenseness of her nerves. It had been hours at the very least that she had remained by the window, leaning against the cool glass, her eyes turned inward in an attempt to search her soul. She loved him. Oh, how she loved him! But she couldn't let him see that. And she couldn't go to him the way he wanted, the way she wanted. She just couldn't do it. Aunt Margaret had instilled her morals too well. She couldn't act as other women her age might—with their freedom. She couldn't take what was offered today and ignore the consequences of tomorrow. She was hopelessly out of date in that regard.

Amanda was pouring cream into her instant coffee when she heard the men approaching the front porch. Her hand began to tremble, but she relaxed slightly as the scrape of chairs signaled they had taken seats outside in order to continue discussing what sounded to be the merits of one breed of cattle over another. Her Uncle Pete, Aunt Eileen's husband, was also a rancher, as were two or three of her distant cousins, none of them having more than a small fraction of the land that Josh possessed. But one quick glance out the window opening onto the porch showed him listening intently to her Uncle Pete's views, respecting the older man's opinion and responding with his own.

Amanda quickly turned her back to the window and sat down at the table, concentrating on her coffee, trying to still the leap of her heart that the mere sight of Josh caused. If she turned even slightly, she would be able to see him; he was positioned in such a way that only the distance across the room, the closed window, and the sheer curtains separated them. His broad, denim-covered shoulders were leaning against the back of his chair, and she could see the crisp vitality of his dark hair and the way it curled down against his collar—if she wanted to turn around, that was; but somehow she didn't need to. His image was forever burned in her consciousness. She knew exactly what he was doing, each movement he made, almost as if she were a part of him.

Clumsily Amanda thumped her cup down, spilling some of the dark liquid on the clean table. She jumped as the door opened and her father entered. Her cheeks flushed at the look she received as she tried inadequately to mop up the spill with her napkin. Her father reached under a cabinet and withdrew some paper towels from a roll and handed them to her wordlessly.

Once she had the mess cleaned up, he eased himself into a chair across from her and said quietly, "Morning, sweetheart."

"Morning, Dad. Would you like a cup of coffee? The water's still hot."

"No, thanks. I've already had some." He watched her take a sip from her cup. "John will be here in a few hours."

"Oh, good. I'm glad. I was afraid he wasn't going to make it."

Her father smiled. "He'll make it. He called this morning. He's chartering a plane and flying down."

Her father became quiet, picking up her spoon and drawing imaginary lines along the wood grain of the table. "Did he talk to you, Amanda?"

At first Amanda had to search her brain for what her father was talking about. Then with sudden clarity she remembered. "Yes, he did."

Her father raised pain-filled eyes to her face. "Did he tell you everything?" At her nod he went on. "In some ways I've never regretted what I did, Andy. It happened,

136

and there wasn't anything your mother or I could do about it. But I've always felt bad about John. And I've sometimes wondered that if she *had* married him—as she might have done if I hadn't entered the picture—she might still be alive today. . . ." Amanda's hand gripped his as his voice died away into nothingness. After a moment he patted it absently, then, clearing his throat, said, "But if that had happened, then you and Marla wouldn't be here, and your mother and I wouldn't have had the happy years that we did." He sighed deeply. "I don't know, honey. Some things in life can seem so simple and yet be so complicated. Then the same thing happens all over again between you and Marla." His blue eyes held her tawny ones. "I thought my heart was going to break when I saw how unhappy you were—and it forced me to really see how John must have felt."

Amanda tried to speak, but her father interrupted. "That was why I called him. I knew if anyone could help you, he could."

"Oh, Dad, I know. You don't have to go on. I know it's hard for you."

"I have to face it sometime, Andy. I've put it off far too long. For years, especially after your mother died, I've had to brace myself to see John. I've always felt as if I took my happiness at his expense."

"But Uncle John's not unhappy, Dad. And he doesn't blame you. He told me so. He doesn't."

"I wish I could believe that." His hand tightened its hold over hers.

Amanda leaned forward, trying to make him understand, her cup of coffee forgotten. "Talk to him, Dad. Talk to him when he comes today. Then maybe you will."

Patrick Reynolds responded to the earnestness in his daughter's voice and looked at her quietly for a long moment before asking, "Do you think so?"

"I know so."

A speculative quality entered his blue eyes. "Are you talking from experience, Andy? Have you found out what I told you you would?"

Amanda's eyes fluttered down to the table, her lashes shadowing her cheeks. "I—I don't know what you mean."

"It doesn't hurt anymore, does it?"

"What?" She was playing for time, and they both knew it.

Her father looked over her shoulder at the masculine form outlined in the window. "I think you know," he answered softly.

Amanda followed his gaze then turned back to face him; all the anguish she was experiencing was there in her eyes for him to see.

"Oh, Dad," she whispered achingly. "It's worse this time. Much worse."

Now it was her father's hand that was doing the comforting. "You left the party early last night," he prompted.

"Yes."

"Want to tell me about it?"

Amanda shook her head, her bottom lip beginning to tremble. "No, it—wouldn't do any good."

Her father was silent for a moment, then said, "I like him, Andy. He's the right kind of man for you." Amanda's startled gaze flew to her father's face. "He's strong in the areas where you need strength and yet he's confident enough in himself to let you have a little room. But he won't let you bully him into doing things your way."

Her father smiled faintly at her protesting look. "You're the oldest, Amanda, and you've always liked having your own way." He paused, and the smile flickered away as he stated, "You love him."

Amanda nodded her head. If it would have solved her problems, she would have thrown herself into her father's

138

arms and clung to him as she had when she was a small child and he could take away all her fears with his comforting touch. But she wasn't a child any longer, and the comfort he could give her wasn't the kind of solace that she needed.

She sniffed loudly. "Is it obvious to everyone?"

"Only to someone who loves you. You give yourself away every time you look at him."

"He doesn't love me, Dad," she whispered, her voice quavering.

Her father squeezed her hand. "He's a deep person, Andy. He doesn't wear his emotions out in the open for everyone to see. Oh, I've seen the way he stands by you in our mob—but that isn't what I mean."

"He doesn't love me," she repeated dejectedly, shaking her head.

"How can you be sure?"

"I know, I just know." How could she tell him what Josh really wanted? And what she had been tempted so often and so sorely to give? She took a taste of her now cool coffee and hoped that the subject could be changed. She had not meant for anyone to know her feelings for Josh, but she should have known that her father would guess. It was inevitable, really; he knew her too well. And if they kept on talking, he would guess the rest—if he already hadn't. But she couldn't discuss it with him. She would have to work things out for herself.

The arrival of the laughing group from upstairs effectively stopped any further conversation, and Amanda shakily got to her feet, asking Marla what she could do to help. She felt her father's eyes on her as she took up the happy chatter with the other women, then gave a mental sigh of relief when he pushed his chair away from the table and declared that if he had to live through another occasion like this too soon, he would be ready for the loony bin, and wandered back outside onto the porch and to the safety of masculine company.

The wedding was set for four o'clock in the afternoon; after the reception, the happy couple would drive to the airport to make their eight o'clock flight to New Orleans.

Marla, tremendously excited at the prospect of a two-week holiday in the Crescent City, ran a worried eye over her suitcase to make sure that she had everything that she wanted to bring: her new vacation clothes; her smuggled bikini, which was so brief, Aunt Margaret would have apoplexy if she saw it; her camera; her array of beautiful night things. But as the day progressed, and the time for the wedding neared, she still showed no signs of nervousness. That was, until forty-five minutes before they were due to leave for the church.

Amanda was in Marla's room, helping put the finishing touches to her sister's hair. Marla had been silent for some time before Amanda suddenly noticed her changed complexion and the panic-filled blue eyes. Hurrying everyone else from the room, she closed the door quietly and leaned back against it. Marla turned slowly on the stool, and said breathlessly, "Andy, I'm afraid. I don't know whether I can do it. I don't know if I love Carl enough. I thought I did, but I don't know now. Oh, Andy!" she wailed, her lovely face crumpling.

Amanda rushed across the polished wood floor to put her arms around her sister's shoulders. A few weeks ago those words might have gladdened her heart, but now all she felt was compassion.

"Hush, sweetheart, hush. Do you want me to call Dad?"

After several loud sniffs, Marla shook her head. "No," she answered huskily. "Oh, Andy, do I love him?" She

140

was almost pleading, looking to her older sister for guidance.

Amanda was taken aback. How could she answer that?

"I mean," Marla continued, "I know you thought you loved Carl once and now you love Josh." Amanda's heart jumped. Did everyone know? "How can you tell the difference?" Marla continued, oblivious to the shock she had given Amanda. "What makes how you feel about Josh any different from how you thought you felt about Carl?"

Troubled, tear-filled eyes searched Amanda's pale face while she cast about in her mind for an answer. There was no use denying her love for Josh; it would only have been a lie, and Marla wasn't looking for any half-truths now. She needed reassurance, and fast.

"I read something once, Marla," Amanda began quietly as she tried to remember the words, "about love in the true sense. It was written by a man, a poet, whose wife had died, and he missed her terribly. I'm not sure if I can remember it exactly, but it went something like this: 'It's not that I am lonely for you— I am mutilated, for you were a part of me.' " Her words fell into a deep silence as Marla absorbed their meaning. "That's the way I feel about Josh. If—when—we have to part, it will be as if my very soul were being ripped from my body. I don't know what will happen . . . afterward."

Marla rubbed her arms as if a chill had just passed over her and stared blankly ahead. Then she sniffed and straightened, moving a strand of her long blond hair away from her face with a shaky hand. She smiled tremulously. "You can let everyone back in now. We don't have much time."

Amanda felt her throat tighten, feeling closer to her sister now than she had in her entire life. As she moved to turn the door handle, Marla halted her with a soft

"Thank you, Andy" that had Amanda almost in a state of tearful happiness.

The wedding was a beautifully simple affair. The small church was packed, and Marla was radiant with glowing happiness. Carl, over the ravages of his previous night's drinking, looked happy, proud, and most of all calm.

The lovely pale orchid dress that Amanda wore matched the pale-orchid frilled shirt of the best man; everything went off without a hitch. No forgotten ring, no fainting of either bride or groom—which Amanda had witnessed at several weddings she had attended in the last few years—no muffled words. The exchange of vows could be heard clearly and concisely throughout the church, and the sealing kiss had everyone smiling. Then came the triumphant rush out of the church and over to the hall that had been rented for the reception.

Following more sedately behind the newly married couple, her arm caught by that of the best man's, Amanda felt her eyes drawn to Josh's. She had been aware of him throughout the ceremony, having spotted him sitting to the rear of the church when she walked down the aisle in preparation for Marla. But she had kept her gaze firmly turned toward the altar, even though she felt the heat of Josh's look. Now she could not avoid it. She faltered as she met his burning gaze; only the hold she had on her companion's arm kept her from falling. The small bouquet of roses and daisies shook in her suddenly trembling hand. He was dressed in a well-cut dark suit with an immaculate white shirt that accentuated his deep tan. His dark hair was well brushed, but part of it fell stubbornly over his forehead, and his strong, virile good looks seemed to make her body throb. Amanda almost cried out at the burning, possessive look that was in his eyes. He wanted her. He intended to have her. And he wasn't going to wait much longer.

All day she had tried to avoid him. Whenever they were forced by whim of the crowd to be in close contact, she had tried to build a wall about herself. At first Josh had been amused, following her evasive tactics with mocking eyes; but later, as she seemed to further close him out, his expression had become cold and withdrawn.

At one time in the day he had disappeared, and for a panic-stricken hour Amanda thought he had left for Craigmont without her. So it was with a surge of relief that she saw him return, driving up to leave the station wagon with a beautifully wrapped package in his hands that bore the stamp of an instantly recognizable exclusive store in Dallas.

Marla had excitedly opened the present and discovered an exquisite pair of crystal vases along with a card that read: WITH OUR LOVE, AMANDA AND JOSH.

At first Amanda had been stunned by his action. Then she became resigned. It was just another way of linking their names together to convince Marla that they were more than just good friends. It was only to herself, deep down inside, that Amanda secretly reveled in the pairing of their names—even if it was just for a little while.

After leaving the church, Amanda didn't see Josh again until a quarter of an hour later. When he came to stand by her side at the reception, his face again had that closed, cold expression, and she wondered if she could have dreamed the hot look of desire he had directed at her earlier. He stayed by her side the entire time, quietly talking to people and answering their questions. But he never more than brushed against her arm or shoulder with the lightest of touches.

After the cake was served and coffee poured, Marla hurried away to change into her going-away dress, a softly feminine creation of pink and white voile. Then when the moment came for the traditional toss of the bridal bouquet to all the unmarried women present, Marla giggled and looked straight at Amanda. Amanda's heart seemed to stop beating as she realized what her sister planned. She didn't want to catch it! Tradition said that whoever caught it would be the next bride, and Amanda knew that that would never happen. Let someone else have the luck. But it was either catch the darn thing or let it fall to the floor at her feet. Marla had always had a good arm. Even in the days before Women's Lib had made it possible for little girls to be a part of little boys' teams, Marla had always been chosen by the boys in town to be their sandlot base-ball pitcher.

A cry of excitement went up when the crowd saw who caught the bouquet, and Amanda felt her face flame with embarrassment. If she could have disappeared from the face of the earth at that moment, she would have—gladly.

Josh's arm tightened its grip around her shoulders when a cry of "When's the date?" filled the air.

Amanda's face brightened even more, if that was possible, as she realized that they weren't asking her but Josh.

Unperturbed, he called back good-humoredly, "We'll let you know."

A responding laugh echoed through the crowd, then their attention was caught by the departing bridal couple and the custom of throwing their handfuls of rice.

Laughing, the couple tried to dodge the well-wishers but failed miserably, becoming almost inundated with the small white grains.

Amanda watched them go, her heart swelling at their happiness; but also sad and afraid that she would never share in such a feeling. Not unless Josh changed. She sighed deeply, a lost, hopeless look snuffing out her smile.

144

Without warning, her lips began to tremble and she had to bite down hard to stop their movement.

A stiffening in the man beside her made Amanda glance around. His face was an unyielding mask, and his silver eyes were hard as he searched her face. On seeing the evidence of unshed tears, his mouth took on a thin, grim look that caused Amanda's forehead to pucker in bewilderment. Why was he looking at her like that? She tried to raise a smile but failed dismally in the presence of his manifest disapproval. In the end she dropped her head and concentrated on the tips of her satin-covered toes—all that was showing of her feet from beneath the long lovely orchid dress.

*CHAPTER NINE*

The idea of not going back to Craigmont entered Amanda's mind more than once during the long night she spent tossing and turning on her narrow bed. The party had gone on for ages after Carl and Marla left, and she had been exhausted with both the strain and the keenly felt nearness of Josh's disturbing presence.

That the townspeople and her relatives believed that it was only a matter of time before they would be receiving an invitation to another wedding was evident in the easy acceptance they showed Josh. No one, not even her closest friends, seemed to remember their earlier pity for her because Carl was marrying Marla. The strong lean figure of Josh Taylor with his compelling masculine presence and quietly commanding air, staying by her side the entire evening and making a statement with his nearness, had had the precise effect he had known it would: It completely silenced all wagging tongues and focused all speculation on himself and his place in Amanda's future.

For Amanda the remainder of the party had been a misery; her main desire had been to get away, to be alone. But once she was alone, she was prey to all the hopes and doubts that had plagued people in love for thousands of years, especially people who loved but knew themselves to be unloved—the most horrible torture known. And she couldn't understand why, though he was always close by her side, she had felt such waves of barely restrained anger and disapproval from Josh.

She awoke the next morning with a pounding headache that even a long hot shower and a couple of strong aspirin did nothing to alleviate. Dark circles were evident under her golden eyes; her normally tanned skin was pale. She had had a bad night, one in a series, and she looked it.

She pulled a pair of new white jeans and a bright yellow T-shirt from her chest of drawers and tried as best she could to cover the evidence of her rough night by applying a heavier amount of makeup than usual. But nothing could be done about the tired droop to her slender shoulders or the shadowed expression in her eyes.

She was afraid to return to Craigmont: the logical side of her brain told her she was only asking for more pain and heartache; but she knew deep inside that she was through with running. Josh had accused her of that once before, and he was right. She did run whenever things became more than she could handle. When she had learned of Carl and Marla's engagement; when she had found for the first time in her life that she had strong physical needs that clamored to be fulfilled; when she had discovered that she loved Josh—she had always run. Now she was tired of running. For once in her life she was going to stand firm and see what fate had in store for her.

That decision had been made sometime in the early morning, before she had finally drifted off into a deep sleep. But the loud slap of a hand on her door and Josh's gruff command that she was to get up—that they had to be on their way—had her resolve crumbling slightly about the edges. It was one thing to build up for a fight in private and another to face an opponent in the ring.

After packing the things she decided to take back with her to Craigmont, Amanda stepped out into the hall. Her head felt as if two warring factions had set up camp and were both trying to best each other in shooting shafts of pain. She winced once when a particularly accurate shot seemed to penetrate her skull, then walked down the stairs in the lull that followed.

Her Uncle John had come for the wedding only and had accepted a lift back to the airport from Josh soon after the reception was over. At first Josh's absence from the room had been a physical release from tension, but later she experienced the same kind of panic as she had earlier in the day when she wondered if he would return. But he had, and he was waiting for her now so that they could begin the journey together.

The farewells to her father and Aunt Margaret were short, her father giving her hand a momentary squeeze and telling her to keep in touch. He then shook hands with Josh, giving him a narrowed-eyed look that the younger man seemed not to notice. Aunt Margaret, much to Amanda's secret amusement, was much in awe of Josh—never once since the time they had first been introduced had she cut into him with her tongue. It was as if she knew a superior adversary when she saw one and contented herself instead with an occasional aggrieved sniff.

Josh seemed to have little to say that morning. Other than a searching glance that stripped away the layers of her carefully applied makeup and a quietly worded "Ready?" he seemed to retreat into himself and concentrate on his driving.

Several times Amanda glanced at him from the corner of her eye—her long lashes screening her probing look—but the stern profile, with its firmly held lips and tightened jaw, revealed nothing.

Was he regretting that he had come? Amanda asked herself, her agitation increasing with each mile they traveled. She had tried to tell him—to warn him. But he wouldn't listen! She rested her tired, aching head against the thick glass of the window and stared outside, a feeling of hopelessness all but swamping her.

When the car slowed down and pulled into the parking. area of a small café, she looked questioningly at Josh. "What's wrong?"

Silver-gray eyes narrowed at her question. "Gas," he replied briefly, motioning to the small island of twin pumps in front of the café.

"Oh," she replied slowly, relaxing her head back against the glass. His impatience to be away from her was obvious.

He got out of the car, his jean-clad legs and hips all that she could see for a moment. Then he bent down. "You want some coffee or something? You didn't eat much for breakfast this morning."

He had noticed! She didn't think he had even been aware that she was in the same room, he had been so coldly remote.

"Er, yes, I—"

"Well, get out, then," he interrupted impatiently. "I'll see about the gas while you go in and order what you want. I'll just have coffee."

Amanda looked at him for a long moment, her eyes revealing her hurt, then she got out of the car and walked with a stiff back toward the double-screened doors of the café.

The waitress, a brunette with a boyishly thin figure dressed in a neat mint-green uniform, was slow in coming. She had just finally got around to taking Amanda's order when Josh walked in and took his seat.

The waitress paused, her bright blue eyes widening in pleased surprise. "Josh? Josh Taylor?"

For the first time that day Josh seemed to come alive. He stared for a moment at the tall, slender woman in uniform, his light eyes narrowing on the pretty oval of her face, then he broke into a slow, crooked smile and got to his feet. "Angel—how are you?"

"It *is* you! Josh!" The woman he had called Angel cried happily and threw herself at him. He caught her in a tight embrace. "It's been so long—so long!" She kissed him uninhibitedly on the mouth before drawing back a space in order to examine his face. "You still look the same. Are all the girls still beating down the brush to get to you, or"—her bright eyes turned, belatedly remembering Amanda's presence—"have you finally gotten caught?"

Josh's harsh features creased in a further semblance of a smile. "Angel, this is Amanda. And, to answer your question, no, not just yet."

Amanda, who was busy trying to fight down the jealous rage that was tearing through her breast at the sight of Josh standing so relaxed with another woman in his arms, nodded jerkily in response to Angel's friendly yet inquisitive smile.

"Well, then, that still leaves hope for me! What are you doing in this part of Texas? I didn't think I'd ever see you again."

Josh seemed perfectly content to keep the woman close, one long arm still around her waist. Amanda's hands clenched under the table, and her teeth positively ground.

"We're just passing through. Amanda is John Reynolds's niece, and I'm taking her back to his place."

*Dismissing me for all the world like an unwanted parcel!* Amanda raged to herself. Her resentful golden eyes flashed up to his mocking face but only had the effect of making his smile deepen.

"Well, you can't leave without coming by to see Teddy. I get a break in another fifteen minutes. Do you think you could wait that long, and come with me to my trailer? It's only about a block away."

A shade of pleading had entered the woman's voice, and

Josh quickly agreed, either not noticing Amanda's restless movement or ignoring it. Angel smiled happily and removed herself from his hold.

"Wonderful!" she declared. "Now, I'd better get back to work or I'll get fired. I'll bring you some coffee, but we'll have something more over at my place. Luckily I made a cake last night—I only hope that Teddy hasn't given it all away to his friends."

She smiled at Amanda's set face and hurried away to collect their cups of coffee. Then she went over to two newly occupied tables and brought out her pad to take the customers' orders.

To Amanda's taste the coffee's flavor was something on the order of river-bottom mud, but as Josh seemed to be enjoying his, his eyes speculatively following Angel's slim figure as she moved from table to table, she knew it was just her own mood. Her jealously was increasing with each passing second and along with it anger at herself for being jealous. Then, to add to her troubles, her headache seemed to increase with vicious intensity.

"An old friend of yours?" she asked sourly, more to get his attention back than to know the answer to the question. Anyone with eyes or ears already knew the answer.

Josh seemed to have difficulty drawing his gaze away from their perusal of the waitress, but he finally turned to Amanda. "You could say that," he drawled, steadily holding her eyes until she was forced to look away.

Amanda sipped at her coffee miserably. It was no use. She could never win a verbal battle with him, and right now she was in no shape to try. Weakly she raised a hand to rub her left temple and winced as a shaft of pain struck. Her head felt as if it were going to explode. She swallowed quickly on a sudden feeling of nausea and felt a thin layer of perspiration gather above her upper lip while at the same time a strange clammy coolness invaded her skin.

With trembling fingers she passed a hand over her mouth, then had to take several deep breaths as the room began to darken. She was going to pass out if she didn't do something, and she had never done anything like that before in her life! Blindly she reached out for Josh, but before she could come in contact with his arm, she felt herself begin to fall.

The grating sound of a chair scraping back was quickly followed by Josh's strong arms coming around her, keeping her upright. Her head lolled onto his shoulder as he asked roughly, "Amanda? What's wrong?"

She gave a low moan in answer before giving herself up to semiconsciousness. She felt Josh's arms tighten about her.

Angel came hurrying over. "What happened? Is she . . . ?"

"Did you say you live close by, Angel?" Josh interrupted tightly, his voice hard.

Angel looked first at the girl lying weakly against him then into Josh's darkened eyes. She nodded slowly. "Just a minute." She hurried over to talk with a man standing behind the counter then came back to Josh, removing her apron and leaving it folded over the back of a chair. "Come on. I'll show you."

Amanda felt herself being lifted into Josh's strong arms and tried to protest. Her head was beginning to feel less woozy. But all she received in response was a briskly ordered "Stay still" as he carried her out the door of the café. His tone tolerated no argument, and Amanda relaxed against his strong muscular frame, one arm going around his neck in meek acceptance.

The trailer was so close, it could be seen from the café, which was located on the outskirts of a small town. Angel ran ahead to open the door, and quickly backed away as Josh mounted the series of steps to carry Amanda inside.

Amanda had a blurred impression of a cramped room cluttered with a small child's possessions and the wide blue eyes of the child as he watched the strange procession go through the room and down the hall. She was lowered gently onto a bed.

Amanda stared dazedly from Josh, sitting on the side of the bed, to Angel, hovering in the doorway. Josh raised one large hand to move aside the cluster of blond curls covering her forehead. His jaw tightened as he felt her skin. "Temperature's up," he grated, as if it were all part of some premeditated plan on her part to cause inconvenience.

Weak tears began to form. She didn't want to feel bad. And she certainly didn't want to make this return trip last any longer than it had to. Ever since last night at the reception he had acted strangely. Had he tired of the whole affair? Did he now wish he were rid of her but felt stuck because he had promised to take her back to her uncle's ranch? Oh, how she wished she had stayed at home! He had played with her emotions from the beginning—he had probably been doing it all along. And she, like a fool, had let him.

"Here, let me see." Angel brushed his hand away. "You know a lot about horses and cattle, Josh Taylor, but I'm beginning to think you know absolutely nothing about women."

Angel reached into a drawer and extracted a thermometer, shook it, and aimed it efficiently toward Amanda's lips.

Too surprised to do anything more than open her mouth, Amanda submitted. After the allotted time, while not another word had been spoken in the room, Angel removed the glass probe and read it, pronouncing satisfactorily, "Just a little above normal. How do you feel now, Amanda?"

Grateful for any show of warmth and concern, Amanda had to sniff loudly to steady her voice. A muscle twitched in Josh's tightly clamped jaw.

"I feel better. I don't know what happened. I've never—"

"I do," Josh interrupted, his voice coldly furious. "I've been with you for days, remember? And I've seen the way you've only played with your food, never eating anything. And I've seen the dark circles under your eyes from not sleeping. Do you still love him that much, Amanda?" he demanded bitterly.

Amanda stared at him with her mouth gaping slightly. What was he talking about? Who was he talking about? Then realization hit. He thought she was still in love with Carl! Was that why he had been so cold and withdrawn since the wedding yesterday? But what had made him change his mind? She racked her tired brain but could think of nothing. "Josh . . ." she began, but was stopped as he stood up suddenly and began to pace the small room.

Angel moved unobtrusively into a corner and watched as the always calm, self-assured man she had known raked agitated fingers through his hair; then, after shooting a blazing look of resentment at the girl on the bed, spun on his heels and left the room.

"Good grief," Angel breathed once they were alone, and turned to look at Amanda, who was still staring blankly at the empty doorway.

Amanda shifted wide, bewildered eyes to the other woman. Angel smiled faintly in response and said, "I've never seen him quite so worked up before. But then again, I've never seen him getting back a little of his own."

Amanda blinked confusedly. "What?"

Angel came toward her and patted her arm. "Never mind, honey. Come on. Let's see if you can sit up."

Later, satisfied that her fainting spell had resulted from

the circumstances Josh had stated, although not exactly for the same reason, Amanda was persuaded to relax against the covers and try with the aid of a couple of aspirin to get some rest. Angel assured her that she would keep Josh occupied, which did nothing to help Amanda relax, but she thanked her anyway and lay quiet in the darkened room.

Sleep never did come; her mind was too active. She kept wondering who Angel was and most of all why Josh had acted in the strange way he had. It was totally out of character for him.

An hour later Amanda was up. Her headache had all but gone away, and she felt as rested as she was ever going to feel until they got back to the ranch and she could get away from Josh. She ran a hand over her hair, making the blond curls bounce, and wished that she had a comb. But since hers was in her purse in the car, she would have to make do. A brush was resting on a low chest only a hand's reach away, but Amanda couldn't bring herself to use it, telling herself she was too fastidious, yet knowing that was not the entire truth. It was, in fact, simple jealousy. The same emotion she had felt earlier upon seeing Josh hold the other woman in his arms. And it returned now with sudden force. Angel was attractive in a slim, athletic sort of way; her features were a little sharp, but she had a smile that instantly warmed a person. And even in her jealousy Amanda had to admit that Angel was kind. Did Josh at one time have a special affection for her? Did he still?

Slowly she made her way down the hall only to pause just outside the doorway to the living room as she heard a voice she recognized as Josh's come from within. He was laughing in that uninhibited way of his that she had heard only once before—soon after she had first met him when he had been the victim of her doctored eggs. Lately there had been no laughter between them, only conflict.

156

Josh laughed again, but this time his laugh was answered by a childish giggle. Curious, Amanda stepped into the room. They were like a family sitting there: Josh on the floor with the small boy sitting at his side and Angel curled up in a chair across from them. Each face had the remnants of good humor—that was, until they looked up and noticed her. Josh's smile died and was replaced by a carefully controlled mask, his silver eyes revealing no emotion. The child was startled by her appearance and looked at her wide-eyed. Only Angel jumped to her feet, apologizing for the noise they had made and the fact that it must have awakened her.

Feeling something like a damp sponge for halting their good cheer, Amanda hastily assured her that that was not the case. She turned her eyes on the child, who was about eight, his brown hair and thin face so like his mother's that there could be no doubt of his relation to her. Angel introduced them.

"Amanda, this is Teddy—my son."

A stiff smile pulled at Amanda's lips. "Teddy."

"Hi," the boy replied, before turning back to his game with Josh.

"Are you feeling better now?" Angel asked, drawing Amanda's attention back to herself.

"Oh, yes. Yes—much."

"Good. Would you like something to eat, then?" Angel motioned toward the small kitchen. "I've made some chicken soup. I thought that might taste good to you. We've already had ours," she added with some embarrassment. "We didn't know how long you would sleep."

"Oh, that's all right," Amanda hastened to reassure her. She wasn't really hungry, but from the intent look Josh was sending her, she would eat if she had to choke over every spoonful. She moved to the narrow table set in a corner of the room and took her place while Angel removed the lid from a steaming pot.

While she ate, Amanda listened to the conversation of the other two adults. She heard them talking about people who lived around Craigmont, people she herself had heard of and sometimes met, and of times in the past when they had been children together—a fact that surprised Amanda, because Angel didn't look to be in her thirties.

Amanda was just finishing her last spoonful of soup when Teddy ran by to find a special toy in his room. Josh shifted his position and calmly lighted cigarettes for Angel and himself.

"You look like you've done all right for yourself since you left Craigmont, Angel. Do you ever regret doing it?"

Angel thought for a moment. "No, I did the right thing." She looked down at the curling smoke of her cigarette, her face thoughtful. "Do you ever see Richard?"

Josh nodded, watching the boyish figure intently. "He's okay. He and Becky have two girls now."

Angel frowned slightly, a look of regret crossing her face only to disappear when Teddy came back into the room, triumphantly carrying a model racing car.

"I'm glad. Is he happy, Josh?" She didn't look at him when she asked the question, her eyes staying on her son.

"I think so."

Angel took a deep breath, as if relieved of a burden long carried. Then she visibly brightened. "You probably didn't notice the man behind the counter, but he owns the café—and, well, he asked me to marry him. We're going to be married in December."

Josh took the rush of news placidly. "Are you sure this time, Angel?"

Angel nodded vigorously, a tremulous smile turning up her lips. "Positive."

158

Josh remained still, reading her face. Then he reached over to kiss her on the cheek.

"Congratulations," he said softly.

Angel grinned and strangely this time, Amanda didn't mind the embrace.

It was late afternoon before Amanda and Josh were able to resume their journey. And for a time Amanda remained silent, her thoughts centered on the woman they had just left, wondering what had remained unsaid in the short conversation that culminated in Angel's announcement of her upcoming marriage. There was a mystery there somewhere. Who was Richard? What role did he play in Angel and Teddy's life? And why had she seemed so relieved that he was now happy?

Amanda chanced a quick look at the hard profile of the man beside her. He, too, had been withdrawn, his thoughts consuming his mind. It was none of her business, really, but she was intrigued. At first she had resented Angel, been jealous of her; but in the end, after hearing of her engagement, she had to admit that she liked her.

She broke the silence by saying, "Angel is very nice." For her effort she received a noncommittal grunt. "Has she been away from Craigmont long?"

Silver eyes darted her a look that warned her not to question him further, that he was in no mood to answer. But Amanda persisted; her need to know was stronger than her heed for caution.

"Who is Richard?" she asked curiously.

At that Josh's displeasure exploded, his fingers gripping the steering wheel tightly as if he wished it were her neck. "You're a spoiled little bitch, did you know that, Amanda? Maybe Carl had a lucky escape." Amanda recoiled as if struck, but Josh continued unrepentant. "I might have known you wouldn't be able to let something like that

159

pass." He shot her a narrow, resentful glance and exasperation tightened his lips. "Richard is a friend of mine. We went to school together. He's also Teddy's father."

Amanda's eyes widened. She should have known. Everything pointed to the fact, but it was still something of a shock.

"Oh!"

"Yes, oh."

"But didn't you say—"

"He's been married to Becky about three years. Teddy was a long time before that."

"I see . . ." Amanda murmured, and thought she did. Teddy must be a love child. That was the reason Angel had to leave Craigmont.

"No, you don't see. Teddy is Richard's legal son."

"But . . ."

"Angel and Richard's marriage was a mistake. I think they both realized it about a month later. They were divorced just after Teddy was born. Then Angel left town with the baby."

Amanda was silent, absorbing what she had been told. Josh continued. "It's a sad story, but it just shows what a mess two people can get themselves into when they jump into something they aren't sure about." He glanced pointedly at Amanda and she realized with a start that he was telling her this for a purpose. He was still going on about herself and Carl! "They're both just now getting their lives in order—only their mistake hurt someone other than themselves. Teddy has never seen his father in all his young life. I'm not about to judge either Angel or Richard —but I'm glad Angel is getting married again, for Teddy's sake as well as her own. The boy needs a father."

Amanda held his gaze for several long seconds, then turned away, curiously shaken. Would she and Carl have ended up in a similar situation if they had drifted along

160

into a marriage? Could she have been left with a child to provide for and too much pride to beg Carl for assistance? It would have been tragic. It *was* tragic. And it was like looking into a magic mirror to see what she might have become if some chance of fate had not snatched the future away from her. The vision was frightening.

# CHAPTER TEN

It was good being back at her uncle's ranch, but even though Amanda had slept soundly for what was left of the night after Josh had dropped her off, she awoke with a restive, uncomfortable feeling. Her head was experiencing what was now a dull, throbbing ache, and her throat felt scratchy and raw. Her energy level was an absolute zero, and even Hazel looked at her consideringly.

"Wedding didn't do you much good," she proclaimed succinctly and with disfavor.

Amanda ran a hand over her forehead, feeling the hot dryness. She must have a little fever again, because she was chilled, though the morning was starting out to be a scorcher. The thermometer hanging on the back porch showed it already to be in the high eighties. She smiled weakly, pulling the edges of her thin cotton robe more closely about her. "I guess it didn't. Do you think I could have a little hot tea? I don't really want anything else."

"Of course, you can." Hazel bustled about the room, gathering cup and saucer and plucking a tea bag from its place in a plastic container. "Do you feel poorly?"

"No . . . not too bad," she lied.

Hazel frowned, her thin face wrinkling more as a result. "Well, I don't think I'll go to my sister's today. I'll stay home to see after you."

Amanda dunked the tea bag into the hot water Hazel had poured. "Oh, no. I'll be fine. You go ahead."

Clearly Hazel was undecided. "I don't know. . . ."

"Hazel!" Amanda put a hand on her hip, trying to convince the woman to take some time off. She had been working constantly since coming home from the hospital. "I'm a twenty-five-year-old woman. I can take care of myself for one day." She smiled teasingly to take the sting out of her words.

"But your uncle said—"

"My uncle has nothing to do with it," Amanda interrupted. "You go ahead. See your sister. Visit Roary. You know he's probably climbing the walls since his leg is coming along so nicely."

"Well . . ." Reluctantly Hazel agreed.

By the time Hazel had seen to all the last-minute chores and found one of the hands who would be willing to make a trip to town, Amanda was really feeling terrible. But she forced herself to see the housekeeper off with a smile and a wave and successfully succeeded in not giving herself away.

All she needed was the bed, she told herself repeatedly as she leaned against the closed door and contemplated the long distance down the hall to her room.

But once in bed she ached so badly in every muscle of her body that she couldn't get comfortable. Weak tears came into her eyes and trickled down onto her pillow. It must be a good case of the flu—she must have been coming down with it yesterday when she fainted. Her throat hurt tremendously each time she swallowed, and she had no way of telling how high her fever had climbed.

She began to waft in and out of sleep, and each time she awakened, Amanda was less sure of her well-being. She seemed to be getting worse. She was cold, then she was hot; when she was hot, she perspired until the thin cotton gown she was wearing along, with the bed sheets, was soaking. Then she would become cold again, and the dampness would add to her misery. If only she could be one way or the other! She didn't know where Hazel kept the winter blankets and she was too exhausted to look. So she lay in the bed with her teeth chattering, huddled under damp sheets, and wondered if possibly she had been too precipitous in encouraging Hazel to take some time off.

The afternoon wore on slowly, and snatches of dreams passed through her mind, visions of the past few weeks: Josh, his searching kisses, his mockery, the burning look in his unusually colored eyes when he wanted her, his kindnesses, his aloofness; Angel; Angel and Josh together; the boy; Marla; Carl. . . . On and on the dreams came. Consciousness was only rarely gained.

It was during one of those short periods of partial reality that Amanda became aware of the sound of her voice hoarsely calling, "No, Carl, no!" She tossed her head from side to side in protest. She didn't want to think about Carl anymore! She didn't want to marry him. If she did, she would look into a glass and become Angel and she knew she couldn't stand Teddy not ever seeing his father—even if she no longer loved him. She wanted to be free! She wanted Josh! But Carl wouldn't let her go!

She fought against the pressure on her arms that was pinning her to the bed.

"Carl!" she croaked in panic. She had to get away! Then slowly, bright fever-glazed eyes opened and focused. The pressure was still holding her to the bed, but she could now see that it was Josh's features hovering darkly over her face.

"My God," he rasped angrily, "what have you done to yourself?"

Amanda tried to answer, but her croaky voice failed her. Instead, she looked at him mutely. She felt the side

165

of the bed give as he lowered his weight onto it, then her hair was pushed aside and a cool hand rested on her forehead.

"You're burning up. How long have you been like this?" When she still couldn't answer, his jaw tightened. "Long enough, from the looks of you." He got to his feet and left the room.

Amanda watched him go with frightened eyes. Was he leaving her like this? Did he hate her so much? Before she could form an answer, he was back, carrying a set of clean sheets over his arm. She followed his movements as he put them down on a chest, then watched with wide eyes as he crossed to the bed and bent down to scoop her up into his arms. Efficiently but gently he placed her in a chair beside the bed.

As if changing bed linen was one of his daily chores, Josh ripped off the damp sheets and replaced them with the clean dry ones. When he was done, he turned to look at her. "Where do you keep your nightgowns?"

Amanda blinked, then motioned toward a drawer. It all didn't seem real somehow. This was just another dream. Josh wasn't here in her room searching through her drawer and extracting a short cotton nightie with clusters of delicate yellow flowers repeated in the pattern.

She watched calmly as he came toward her. If this was a dream, it would go away now, but it didn't. She came to her feet when he half lifted her and shivered as he drew the damp clinging gown over her head.

"Pretend I'm Carl," Josh muttered darkly as he threw the worn gown to the floor and settled the fresh one onto her shoulders.

When it was in place, he scooped her up once again and placed her between the sheets. A series of uncontrollable quakes rippled over her and her teeth clattered together helplessly. Josh looked down into the pleading wide eyes, then he disappeared again only to return with several heavy blankets.

After a while Amanda finally managed to become warm. Meekly she took the tablets Josh gave her with a glass of water and soon drifted off into a more comfortable sleep.

When she awakened again, it was to find that her head was clearer and the room was almost in total darkness. The blankets were off her now, only the sheet remained, and she was warm with dampness. But it was a different kind of warmth, and she knew that her high fever had broken. She turned her head slowly and saw Josh sitting in the bedside chair. So it hadn't been a dream. He had come to help her. But how had he known? His head was leaning back against the cushion and his eyes were closed; his arms were crossed and his legs extended straight out toward the bed. He was sleeping, or at least that was what she thought until he sat up with a jerk and looked at her with intent gray eyes.

When he saw that she was awake, he reached over to feel the side of her face. "Better, but you still have a little fever. Can you talk now?"

Amanda swallowed experimentally. Her throat still hurt, but it was much better. When she tried, she found that she could even talk, although huskily. "Yes."

He leaned back and searched her face. "Okay. Then tell me where Hazel is."

"She's at her sister's."

"When did she leave? Didn't she know you were sick?"

Amanda answered only one of his questions. "I told her I'd be fine. I wasn't—"

Josh partially stifled an expletive as he abstractedly ran a hand through his dark hair. "Dammit, Amanda!"

Ridiculously Amanda found herself apologizing. "I'm sorry, Josh. I'm sorry. . . ."

Josh's jaw was clenched tightly shut as he muttered grimly, "Not any more than I am. Come on. I've got to get those sheets changed again. You've picked up some kind of virus, and we have to keep you dry."

Amanda submitted once again to being lifted from the bed and placed in the chair. Then, when the sheets were changed and Josh had found her last remaining nightgown, she felt her face begin to burn. He had helped her once before, but somehow that had been different. Not quite meeting his eyes as he came to stand before her, she breathed, "I can manage, thank you."

She held out a hand, silently cursing the weakness that made even that an effort. Whether it was a combination of her still-ill state or the thought of him undressing her once again, she didn't know. She didn't even know if she could stand.

Josh paid absolutely no attention to her request. He stood her up, removed her gown, and replaced it with the other, all with the efficiency of a designer working on a mannequin.

When she was back between the sheets, she couldn't help the resentful look she shot him. He saw it but smiled mockingly.

"I'm going to take your temperature. Then after that I want you to take a little of the drink I'm going to mix for you."

"One of your concoctions for a cow?" she asked sweetly.

"I ate your eggs," he reminded her. It was a low blow for someone who was ill. Amanda's chin dropped and she kept it down until he had left the room.

After finding that her temperature was only a half a degree above normal and discovering that the mixture he pressed onto her tasted pleasantly of honey and lemon with a dash of whiskey, Amanda felt more like a human being. She was still weak, but she didn't hurt anymore.

"When is Hazel going to be back?" Josh asked, interrupting her thoughts.

Amanda's grip on the sheet tightened. She didn't want to tell him; she didn't know how he would react—but he would find out soon enough anyway, so she thought it best to tell him the truth. "She's spending the night."

No appreciable change came over his features. It was as if he had known the answer already. "And you were going to stay here all alone—as sick as you were." It was a statement, not a question.

Amanda slowly nodded. "But I wasn't that sick when she left."

"Why didn't you call me? You know I—" He stopped there, not finishing his sentence.

Amanda looked at him curiously. "You what?"

"Forget it." He sighed heavily. "I can't bring you home with me, Amanda. I can't risk exposing my mother to what you have; her condition's too delicate. So I'll have to stay here. You can't be alone. You might have a relapse." When he had finished, he shot her a challenging glance that dared her to raise an objection.

Amanda stared at him, remembering the last time he had stayed the night with her in this house and what had ensued. She moved uneasily in her bed.

"Don't worry, honey," he remarked nastily. "I don't intend to rape you. Even I draw the line at that."

Amanda's face whitened at his brutality. What was the matter with him? Ever since the night of the wedding it seemed he had changed. Tears began to pool in her eyes. Damn him! Why did she always seem to dissolve into tears whenever he spoke harshly to her? Determinedly she willed herself to stop. She'd be damned if she would let him see how much he could hurt her with his words. She

169

swallowed tightly and replied stiltedly, "I feel much better now. You can stay if you want or leave. It doesn't make the slightest bit of difference."

Anger burned in the silver eyes as his lean jaw clamped stubbornly shut. "All right," he clipped. "If that's the way you want it. I'll go."

Airily Amanda dismissed him, all the while dying a little inside. "Whatever. . . ."

The room was quiet after Josh left. Amanda had not really believed he would leave until she heard the back door slam shut and the sound of a car's engine start up and race away. Then it was everything she could do not to dissolve into an ocean of tears. Oh, she hated him! Stubborn, arrogant, hateful man! Leaving a sick person. Listening to one!

Then she stopped. There was no use trying to fool herself. She loved him and she always would. No matter how he treated her, she would love him.

Surprisingly the orgy of tears did little to make her feel any worse. In fact, in some way it helped. It was as if she had been released from some tightly held tension and was now free. She had come to a crossroad in her life and could see clearly that she had two distinct choices: She could run away—go somewhere else to start a new life—or she could stay here and use the attraction she knew Josh felt for her to her advantage—take a chance on his coming to love her.

Deep in her heart Amanda knew what her decision was going to be. She would stay. She would stay and fight.

With a sigh of contentment she relaxed against her pillow. Yes, she felt much better now. Maybe it was just a cold after all. And in a few days she would be back to normal and she could begin her siege. General William T. Sherman, who marched through the South to the sea during the Civil War, would look like a rank amateur in comparison with Amanda and the way she would run her battle plan. And she had a few secret weapons in her arsenal that General Sherman hadn't possessed.

## CHAPTER ELEVEN

Several days later, when Amanda was feeling completely well again, she found that it took a certain amount of cooperation from the victim for the assailant to attack— he had to be at least in the vicinity! And Josh was not. He had gone to Houston on business, Megan Taylor told her when she called. The older woman had looked at Amanda's shocked face curiously, but diplomatically asked about the wedding, requesting to be told all about it.

Amanda's return trip to her uncle's ranch had been a slow one. Josh was gone—and she didn't know for how long. His mother had said he left Tuesday morning, which was the day after she sent him away. That he hadn't waited to see how she was recovering jolted her but didn't weaken her resolve.

He couldn't be gone very long. He had his ranch to look after and was still keeping a managerial eye on Uncle John's until Roary's return. He was needed here too desperately to be away for any length of time.

With a catch in her voice that she tried to disguise with a cough, she carefully brought up the question of his return with Hazel. The housekeeper had appeared early Tuesday morning, stating in no uncertain terms that she was back and that she would take no arguments from Amanda as to the care Hazel knew she needed.

The housekeeper, cleaning vegetables for their midday

meal, frowned slightly before replying, "Well, you see, he's a lot like your uncle in the way he runs his ranches. He puts good men in as foremen—especially the one near Houston. Then he's free to do as he wants. But I will say this for Josh. He stays busy. Whichever ranch he's on—which is mostly the one here—he works right along with his hired hands. No long-distance operation for him. And he's always willing to help the people that live around here. Just like he did your uncle when Roary and I had our accident, and John was away at that art thing. He's a good man, Josh Taylor. Too bad some woman can't find the key to his heart."

Amanda's eyes widened at the series of revelations. That Josh owned more than one ranch was a shock. She had thought the neighboring one to be his only possession. Lord knew it was large enough. What was the one near Houston like? And the second shock was that Hazel had a romantic streak. "Key to his heart"—it was almost poetic!

"How long does he usually stay down in Houston?" Amanda tried to sound unconcerned, but Hazel's lips quirked as she kept her head bent to her job.

"Oh, sometimes a month, sometimes two." Amanda's heart sank. "But lately, with his mother being so bad off, he doesn't usually stay but a week or two at the very most."

All that time! Amanda's nerves jerked in protest. Maybe by then he wouldn't want to see her again. But then she remembered his huskily spoken "You're mine, Amanda," which he had proclaimed so proprietarily. And she felt a little comforted.

The following week seemed endless, and Amanda filled it with a multitude of drawings of the ranch house, of the small and large buildings in the outer yards, of scenery and cattle, and of the hired hands as they worked. Once she had even persuaded Roary, who had returned as foreman in a limited capacity, to let her sketch him; but it had not turned out to be successful. Roary was a small, wiry man with a face that could completely change itself around according to his mood. He was as hard to capture as quicksilver, and she wondered if her uncle had ever thought to accept the challenge. She would have to ask him the next time she spoke to him. He knew she was back; he called at least every second day, and her father kept the telephone company in business by his frequent calls. It was as if they were worried about her—and not without cause, she admitted, when she remembered what she had told her father and what her uncle had been able to see for himself at the wedding. It had probably come as something of a shock to see his niece being led about by his neighbor. He had made no comment that she knew of, just speculated, along with everyone else.

She made friends with some of the horses but never attempted to ride one. She was one Texas girl who would probably go to her grave without ever having mounted a horse, if she had anything to say about it, that was. They were beautiful animals, but as far as she was concerned, they were there only to be looked at and petted. As Aunt Margaret would say, "God gave mankind two good legs and the intellect to discover the wheel"—and she was satisfied with that.

Most evenings Amanda would visit Megan Taylor, not only to feel closer to Josh by being with his mother but also out of a growing love for the gentle woman herself. On the evenings she didn't visit her, she would sit in her room going over the larger drawings she had made from her original sketch of Josh. She wished she could paint it in oils but knew it was beyond her skills at the present. Maybe one day.

One afternoon at the beginning of the second week, she had gone into her room earlier than usual and was sitting staring at one of her larger drawings of Josh when she heard his voice. At first she didn't believe her ears, but when she caught Hazel's reply, she knew that Josh was back. Hastily gathering all the drawings together and placing them in a protective folder, Amanda checked her appearance in the mirror, straightening the collar of her blue plaid shirt and fluffing up the natural curls of her blond hair. She was breathless when she ran into the kitchen, her golden eyes alive with excitement, only to discover that he had gone.

Hazel looked at her with something like pity as she saw the bright smile falter and disappear.

With a nonchalance she didn't feel, Amanda stuffed her trembling hands into the pockets of her skirt and asked, "Was that Josh I heard?"

"Yes. He—er—he came to bring something Roary needed."

"He—he didn't stay?"

"No. Said something about having brought company home."

Amanda's stomach fell to the floor. Company. A woman?

"Oh, well, thanks. I—I think I may drive over there later." She would have to find out, and the sooner the better. If it was a woman, it would be the end. He would be telling her loudly and clearly that everything was over between them—what little there had ever been.

She turned away from Hazel but knew that any sort of pretense was useless with the observant housekeeper. That good woman had her finger in everything that happened around the ranch and nothing could be kept from her for long—especially now that she had taken Josh's advice and had her hearing aid repaired.

"You do that," Hazel replied bracingly, turning back to her ironing.

It took a lot of courage for Amanda to drive her Volkswagen over to Josh's ranch, especially when he had earlier shown such little curiosity about her well-being. It was almost as if he were intent on ignoring her, or worse, had already forgotten her completely!

Her heart was beating wildly when she turned into the familiar entrance to the ranch. As she drove down the long road and approached the house, she saw a group of men standing beside a corral near the barn. After a hasty swallow she decided to take her courage in hand and join them—she could see Josh's tall form in their midst.

Josh looked up at the sound of her car door closing to see her coming toward them. Even at that distance Amanda could feel the impact of his silver eyes. She stopped. With a word to those around him, Josh broke away.

"You lived, I see," he stated as he ambled to a halt before her.

If that was a greeting, she was not prepared for it.

"What do you want, Amanda? I'm busy."

He was so close she had only to reach out a hand to touch him. But she didn't. All her careful planning flew out of her mind as she watched his closed expression amazedly.

"Is that all you have to say to me?" she squeaked. "That you're busy?"

"What else do you want me to say?" The anger was now revealed deep in his eyes. "You pretty well told me where I could go the last time I saw you—and believe me, I've been there."

New lines of strain had sharpened the creases on both sides of his mouth, and his face had a drawn look, but Amanda was too beside herself with anger to notice. All

her plans! And he had crushed them with several carelessly spoken words.

"As far as I'm concerned, Josh Taylor," she spat out,
both hands coming to rest on her hips and her chin elevat-
ing itself in defiance, "you could have *stayed* there!" She
stomped one foot childishly, then turned and ran back to
her car, tears of anger and humiliation blurring her vision.
All her carefully laid plans—trampled in the dirt at his
feet! And the most horrible thing about it was that he
didn't even know. Oh, God! Why had she ever had to meet
him in the first place?

In spite of her trembling Amanda got the car started
and raced out of the yard, dust billowing up behind the
back wheels, sending out a cloud toward the men near the
barn. She saw the result of her action in her rearview
mirror, but for once didn't care.

The distance from Josh's ranch to the Double L usually
took about thirty minutes to drive, but Amanda made it
in fifteen. She had driven along the narrow, graded road
like a wildwoman, no longer caring what fate had in store
for her.

When she reached the house, she stopped with a screech
of brakes and jumped out into a gathering cloud of dust
that almost choked her. Without a thought for anything
else she ran to her room and started to throw her few
possessions into a suitcase. She was in a frenzy to get
away. If he didn't want to see her again, she would leave.
But she was not running away. She wasn't! She was just
leaving—in a quickly decided rush. She didn't want to
ever see him again, to subject herself to his cutting tongue.
She had been crazy to think he might ever come to care
for her, that she could make him love her. Crazy! All he
had ever felt for her was a passing physical desire, and at
her age she should have known that some men would tell
a woman anything to get what they wanted. That had been

what Josh had done. Just because he had told her that she was his. . . . She never was his, and she never would be. She had seen it in the cold glance he had run over her as he walked toward her from the corral. He didn't even want to know her now! He had told her once before that he gave no second chances. Now she knew he meant it. But strangely she couldn't find it in herself to feel any sense of triumph because she had held out against him. She just felt sick inside and knew that it would be a long time before she was truly well again—if ever.

After stuffing all of her clothing into a suitcase, Amanda turned to her folder holding the sketches. She didn't have enough time now to destroy those of Josh. She would bring them with her and do it later. She didn't want any evidence of her folly to be left lying around.

Hazel looked after her flying figure and called to her, but Amanda was too upset to answer. She didn't even notice the dark gathering of clouds or hear the ominous sound of thunder as it rumbled in the distance.

Her little car started on the first try, and she raced down the drive, turning toward Craigmont. She didn't know where she was going, but it was not home to Kemperville. People there knew about Josh, and that would as effectively banish her from their presence as their onetime pity for her about Carl. She wouldn't be able to answer their questions or deal with their unspoken speculations as to why she had now lost Josh as well.

The speedometer on the car was pushing seventy when Amanda let up on the pedal and allowed the Volkswagen to slow down. There was no use trying to kill herself or inadvertently kill someone else, and that was precisely what could happen on this narrow road that was sometimes frequented by drivers who were as apt to use the middle as they were to drive on the correct side.

Amanda didn't notice the rapid darkening of the sky

until a brilliant flash of lightning lighted up what seemed to be the entire world. It was soon followed by a reverberating crash. For an instant she completely let up on the accelerator; then, gaining control of herself, she reapplied pressure. It was a bad storm and she was going directly into it, but it was no worse than the storm she had just left behind. Her hands clutched the steering wheel so tightly that her knuckles whitened, and she had to clamp her teeth together to keep from crying out—but she was going to go on.

And go on she did. The rain came down in sheets, and the wind almost blew the small car off the road, but Amanda forced herself to continue, although it was at a snail's pace in comparison to her earlier speed. Then once again a spectacular flash rent the night-dark sky and Amanda jerked her hands from their taut handling of the car to cover her eyes. Before she knew what was happening, she had lost control and the car was coming to an abrupt halt at a precarious angle in a ditch.

For a few seconds Amanda sat in stunned stupefaction, not knowing what had happened. Outside, the storm still raged and seemed to grow even stronger. Amanda slowly sank down into her seat to cover her head, her overcharged emotions during the last few hours coming together to make her a trembling mass of fear. All she had needed was a storm to complete her day! She laughed out loud at the thought, but it was not a pleasant sound. It soon ended on the beginnings of another clap of thunder.

What must have been ages later, but was probably in reality only a long succession of minutes, Amanda felt the passenger door of the car jerk open, and she looked up, startled. She jumped convulsively when she saw it was Josh. He was dripping wet, his hair plastered down over his face and neck, and he was wearing his bright yellow rain slicker. He hurriedly folded his length into the cramped seat, slammed the door shut, and turned to her, all expression absent from his face. He searched her ghost-pale features and looked deeply into her golden eyes then groaned and allowed the torture that had been building in him finally to have its release. He pulled her against him, wetness and all, and Amanda gladly went.

"Oh, God, Amanda. I can't take it anymore!" he rasped achingly.

"Josh!" Amanda breathed, hugging him close. Water was dripping from his hair down onto his shoulders and consequently onto her, but Amanda didn't care. He was here, and he was holding her!

"Amanda—" His voice broke as he began to kiss her hair, her temples, her eyes, and finally her mouth, hungrily, as if he were a dying man and had been granted his one last wish.

The urgent beat of his heart as he crushed her to him drove all fear from Amanda. The heavens could fall for all she cared—just so long as she remained here in Josh's arms.

After a long moment he reluctantly moved to put her away from him. A quick glance outside showed that the rain had slackened. It was still coming down but not with the vengeance it had been. Josh said, "Come on," and pulled her fully onto his lap; then wrapping the voluminous folds of the rain slicker about her, he carried her to the station wagon, protecting her exposed head and shoulders with his body as best he could.

Leaning into his car, he placed her on the seat. He bent down and kissed her quickly. "Stay here. I'll get your things." Amanda watched him disappear once again into the rain.

When he came back, he put her suitcase on the backseat and carefully withdrew the folder from within his slicker, placing it to one side. Several of the drawings slipped out, but he quickly put them back in.

He started the car without speaking, but Amanda didn't mind. His eyes when he looked at her said everything, and she was no longer afraid for the future. Whatever happened now was left to him. If he wanted her, she was his—no matter how he phrased the proposition.

They didn't speak during the entire drive to the ranch, and Amanda was content just to be near him; words were suddenly unnecessary. But when he passed her uncle's ranch and kept driving down the road toward his own, she made a small sound that caused him to turn to her. "I'm taking you home," he explained softly.

If Amanda's soul could have soared at that moment, it would have. She was so tired of the battle, the uncertainty, and the word *home* as he had spoken it sounded like heaven.

It was still raining when Josh drew up in front of his house, and Amanda was transported in the same manner as she had been from her car: held tightly in his arms and protected as if she were a delicate piece of porcelain that was too precious to lose.

When the massive front door opened to his touch, Amanda was surprised to see that the room contained a group of people; some of them were holding drinks, and the television evening news was blaring.

To say that the men were surprised was also an understatement. But Josh didn't seem to mind. He just grinned at them, looked down at Amanda's slightly dampened curls, and kissed her soundly in front of them all.

Amused laughter greeted his action along with a jokingly worded "That's the way to keep her in line, son," as one of the men recognized her as the girl who had a short while before left so precipitously.

Josh heartily agreed, his gray eyes mocking yet tender.

Then he said, "Gentlemen, if you'll excuse us for another few minutes, I might be able to introduce you to the future Mrs. Josh Taylor. But first I have to convince the lady."

Shouts of encouragement followed them down the hall. Josh still had not put her down, and Amanda wondered if he was ever intending to—not that she cared. It was wonderful being held close in his arms, feeling his strength, breathing his heady male scent.

When he had closed the door of his office behind them, he released her only long enough to remove his wet slicker, leaving it a heap on the floor. Then he gathered her back up against him and sank down into a wide leather chair. For a moment he just looked at her, silver flashes in his unguarded eyes showing his love and desire and the determination that this time she was not going to run away. Then he began to kiss her hungrily, mindlessly, and an answering desire exploded recklessly through Amanda's veins. She pressed herself against him, feeling the hardness of his body, feeling the heat of his need.

"Woman, I love you," he breathed unsteadily when at last their lips parted.

Amanda, working hard to control her breathing as well, replied shakily, "I didn't think I'd ever hear you say that."

Josh raised one eyebrow. "Why? You must have known I was crazy about you." He kissed her again to prove the validity of his words, only this time the kiss was short and gentle.

In spite of this it took Amanda some time to recover. When at last she did, she denied it. "No, I didn't. I thought you . . . well, that you just wanted me."

A becoming tinge of pink entered her cheeks as she admitted this, and Josh chided her softly, "But I do want you."

"Oh, I know! And I'm so happy I could . . . But you know what I mean. I thought you just wanted an affair.

183

And then I thought that you didn't want to have anything more to do with me. That's why I was leaving." She tightened her hold around his neck and buried her cheek against his shoulder, enjoying his nearness, his warmth. "I love you so very much, Josh."

His arms tightened, and for a moment Amanda thought she was going to be crushed; then he moved to put a hand under her chin in order to raise her face so that he could look at her. The old amusement was back in his eyes, only now it was accompanied by a tender new light.

"You've led me one hell of a dance, woman. Sometimes I didn't know whether I was up or down." Amanda's golden eyes widened. *He* didn't know whether *he* was up or down! "And I was so jealous of Carl that I forced my way into accompanying you to the wedding, and then when we got there and you seemed to go out of your way to avoid me—and whenever you couldn't, you seemed to freeze—well, let's just say that I could cheerfully have killed you. *Both* of you. Especially at the reception when you almost cried as Marla and Carl left. I began to wonder if you'd ever admit to yourself that you didn't love him."

"But I didn't!" Amanda denied hurriedly. "I knew it then. At one time I thought I loved Carl, but I found out right after I met you that I didn't."

Josh nodded, tracing a finger over the outline of her soft lips, his eyes darkening at the contact. "You certainly didn't respond to me as if you loved someone else. That's why it was such a shock when your uncle told me about Carl." He paused as if remembering the past, then went on. "I knew I could make you want me—physically, sexually—but this time, for the first time in my life, that wasn't enough."

"I love you, Josh," she assured him softly, watching him with a gentle, loving expression.

"I know that—now."

A thoroughly satisfying kiss followed, only to be encored by another and another . . . and it was some time later before Amanda was able to straighten her blouse, reattach its loosened buttons, and smooth down the crumpled hem of her skirt.

As she did she asked casually, "Josh, why did you go away last week?" It still hurt that he had left her when she was ill and he had never tried to find out whether she recovered.

Josh sighed and ran a hand through his dark hair that Amanda had so recently riffled. "I had to get away from you, honey. Like I said, my feelings were so strong, they bordered on hate. It was eating me up inside that you didn't love me."

"But you never called. And you left me that night. I told you I didn't care if you went or not—but I did, Josh."

Josh kissed her lightly in apology. "I know. And I didn't go far. I spent the night in the bunkhouse."

"But I heard the car drive away."

"Only down to the gate. I walked back. I couldn't leave you all alone and sick. The next morning I called Hazel, and she kept me posted as to how you were doing."

"She did?" Amanda asked incredulously.

Josh nodded. "I acted as if it was only because I was looking after you for your uncle, but I think she figured me out."

Amanda giggled. "She had me pegged too. She told me some woman needed to find the key to your heart."

"You have it."

Now it was Amanda's turn to express her thanks to him. Shyly yet confidently she pressed her lips to his in a soft, sweet kiss.

"When will you marry me, Amanda?" he asked huskily at its end.

Amanda smiled and teased, "Is tomorrow too soon?"

"Not for me."

She laughed softly, then a sobering thought caused her to frown slightly. "Do you want a big wedding, Josh?"

"Not particularly, no. But remember what that man said at the wedding. His wife's always regretted that they eloped. I don't ever want you to regret anything about our marriage."

"I wouldn't, even if it were the simplest of ceremonies in a justice of the peace's office. But there's your mother, Josh; and my dad—and Hazel. Hazel would never forgive us if we just turned up one day married."

"That she wouldn't. Well, I guess it's settled then. A big wedding."

"Does it have to be big?" she ventured, looking up at him from under long, curling lashes. "Couldn't we just have our families and close friends? That way it won't be too much of a strain on your mother."

Nothing she did or said could make Josh love her more, but that question almost did. He hugged her to him and throatily whispered, "Just don't make me wait too long, that's all."

Amanda burrowed her face against his neck, feeling his throbbing pulse. "One month?" she questioned expectantly.

"One month," he agreed. "But that's all." Then suddenly he began to laugh. "We've forgotten my guests. But since they already think I'm half crazy, it won't matter much. When you left in such a hurry, I was in no shape to care what any of them thought."

Amanda looked at him suspiciously, remembering that at the time her visit had been to see if his house guest was a woman.

"Those men in the living room?"

Josh nodded. "They're some cattle buyers from Houston."

"All male?"

"As far as I know, unless you had me so confused I didn't notice the difference. Why?"

Amanda gave a small secret smile and replied easily, shrugging. "I just wondered."

Josh slowly began to lower his head. "Well, stop wondering. I'm the only male I want you to be concerned with from now on—unless somewhere on down the line we're lucky enough to have a son."

## LOOK FOR NEXT MONTH'S
## CANDLELIGHT ECSTASY ROMANCES™

84   LOVE HAS NO MERCY, *Eleanor Woods*
85   LILAC AWAKENING, *Bonnie Drake*
86   LOVE TRAP, *Barbara Andrews*
87   MORNING ALWAYS COMES, *Donna Vitek*
88   FOREVER EDEN, *Noelle Berry McCue*
89   A WILD AND TENDER MAGIC, *Rose Marie Ferris*

# When You Want A Little More Than Romance—

# Try A Candlelight Ecstasy!

## The unforgettable saga of a magnificent family

# IN JOY AND IN SORROW

### by JOAN JOSEPH

They were the wealthiest Jewish family in Portugal, masters of Europe's largest shipping empire. Forced to flee the scourge of the Inquisition that reduced their proud heritage to ashes, they crossed the ocean in a perilous voyage. Led by a courageous, beautiful woman, they would defy fate to seize a forbidden dream of love.

**A Dell Book**       **$3.50**       **(14367-5)**

---